Matriarca

Jodi Clark

Published by Lulu

Copyright © Jodi Clark, 2012
All Rights Reserved

ISBN 978-0989120746

Chapter 1

"Ladies and gentlemen, please remain seated until the aircraft is in the air," the friendly voice of the airline stewardess announced as I settled in for my long flight. Friendly, it was an emotion that I had, so effortlessly, misplaced through the years. In my world, there was simply no place for it. Where I came from, being friendly was the difference between life and death. My lifestyle had made me dangerous from a very young age, and everything that I knew had been bred into me by my Sicilian father, Lorenzo.

Most of my childhood memories involved a frequent crowd of the same people – Uncle Anthony, Gino, Mario – authentic, pure-blooded Sicilians, flawlessly clad in perfectly pressed suits and ties, who demanded respect and flashed wads of one hundred dollar bills as if they were ones and fives. Their wives were outspoken souls of silicone and plastered makeup under widely teased manes who arrived in fur coats and spike heels, emitting a blended aroma of cheap perfume and whatever dish they carried in with them. To most who knew or even knew of them, these people were high rollers, icons of society who were both powerful and respected. To me, they were family.

We were a very tight and secluded group, twenty or thirty of us crammed around the table for dinners every week with one boisterous voice always overtaking another with banal jokes and the roars of laughter that ensued. I, of course, was always stuck at the smaller table with all of the kids, my cousins, a daunting task since I realized early on that they were nothing like me. It was always as if I was different, almost foreign, to the others my age. I didn't seem to fit in with the girls, meticulously making over one another's hair and nails, or the boys playing ball outside. Neither was my thing. After dinner, the brash, gossiping women cleaned up while the men always retreated to the den with their cigar-filled conversation, business, as they referred to it and, for some reason, with them is where I always preferred to be and I would've had I been welcome.

I was nine years old when I began to notice how much power my father truly had among others. It was then that I started to see the supreme respect that everyone had for him, the way that my "uncles" always consulted him on nearly every decision they made and how my traditionally valued mother obeyed his every command, but it didn't stop there within our home. We were treated like monarchs everywhere that we went, from the gun shop to church, and my father was greeted with both honor and fear combined. No matter where we were, he was deemed royalty. He appeared to have some sort of interest in everyone and everything, and I swore that he owned nearly every building in town.

"Dad, what kind of business do you do?" I once probed, yearning to know his secret, the thing that kept him out all hours of the night, in secrecy, away from my mother and me, the thing that delivered him such reverence and yielded him the power of a king.

After a brief glare, he put his arm around my shoulder with a faint smirk. "I'm the capo", he casually replied which, in our language, meant that he was the boss. "I tell my employees what to do and they do it." His response was short-lived and left a lot to the imagination but, for me, it was enough. They were words of freedom and I knew, at that moment, that I wanted to be just like him. He was the epitome of influence and I gazed at him in admiration.

I began observing him more closely, studying his movements, his demeanor, the very words that he uttered, so much so that my mother's most frequent phrase to me became, "you're just like your father" and, though her words were never intended as a compliment, they always filled me with pride. I suppose it was an aggravation to see me following in my father's footsteps rather than hers. Young Sicilian girls like me were groomed to be subservient housewives and mothers, bred to cater loyally to our husbands and children, but I refused to settle for a lifestyle that I didn't want, one that was of no interest to me. I craved the exhilaration and influence that was my father's world.

I suppose the first significant realization that I wasn't the average girl surfaced at twelve years old when I noticed a complete lack of interest in hair and makeup, sleepovers and boys. I began to see the colossal difference between myself and other girls my age. While they were giving one another makeovers and aspiring to be perfect housewives, I was making money, hustling the boys in the neighborhood out of their weekly allowances, racking up hundreds of lira a day, which I stashed in my tiny bedroom closet. Even at that age, the game was easy for me. I was a natural at winning their money through games and bets, and it soon became a competition between the boys to determine who my best challenger was. To the girls in my school and neighborhood, I had become a source of intimidation, a freak of nature, not conforming to what girls were supposed to be. Because I wasn't like them, I didn't like them, they assumed, no matter how cordial I always strove to be, and they didn't particularly care for me either because I was intimidating and different. My aggressive personality plagued me an outcast among my female peers. With them, I was always far out of my element and, as time went on, they all just assumed that I was a lesbian. High school was proving to be just a social arena of cliques, none of which I was a part of and, truth be told, my plan was to drop out when I was sixteen so that I could make money full time.

At fifteen, my art evolved as I discovered additional ways

of earning money, aside from my poker playing abilities within the neighborhood. I began to buy things cheap, things that the neighborhood kids wanted – bikes, skateboards and such at local garage sales, refurbished them and then sold them for cheaper than the stores and shops. It was a newfound business that was an instant success and I was doubling my money on most occasions. Already, I had enough to buy myself a car.

"Where did you get all of this money?" My mother demanded to know while summoning my father to discipline me. "Tell me right now how you got all of this! Have you been stealing?" It was just like her to assume that a girl couldn't earn it on her own.

"No, Ma, I earned it." I explained to my parents how I bought and refurbished things to resell, and both of their faces housed an obvious sign of bewilderment. They hadn't expected this out of me. Neither seemed prepared for what they heard and they appeared uncertain as to how to respond.

"You what?" My mother looked horrified in the midst of her confusion. She turned to my father for a solution. His faint smirk revealed a sense of pride as he peered down at me.

"How much money have you made from this?" was all that he said at that moment.

"What does that matter?" My mother piped in once again. "She's scamming these kids out of their allowances and pay from their summer jobs." The thought of her daughter pioneering her own life was clearly appalling to her.

"It's not that bad," he rationalized with veiled approval in his eyes and it was to my relief since my father's temper was never well hidden. "She's not doing anything illegal and those kids know what they're paying for. It's genius, really, and I gotta say, I'm impressed." There it was, the old man was actually proud of my entrepreneurial skills.

"That's it? That's all you're going to say about it?" My concerned mother quipped. "What am I supposed to tell their mothers?"

With his arm around me and a shrug of his shoulders, his

response was, "tell them they should've had smarter kids," and both of us snickered at his joke, though my mother didn't seem to find much humor in it. "Come on, leave the kid alone," he told her while guiding her out of the room. I was stunned that I had been let off the hook so easily by my parents and it meant that I could continue in my venture.

Later that day, I approached my father again, who was in his recliner reading the newspaper. Since I had found myself in his good graces earlier in the day, I decided to try my luck again. "I want to buy a car," I announced.

"You're not old enough to drive," he replied calmly, peering for a mere second overtop of his reading glasses.

"I'll be sixteen in two weeks," I calmly reminded him.

"Right, so you can get one then," he said and returned to his paper. That was always my father, forthright and rigid. He was quick-tempered and set in his ways, and no one who knew him ever argued with his decisions. In our family, there was never any question about who was in control. He wore the pants.

With my birthday rapidly approaching, my mother was steadily making plans for the massive gala that was traditionally thrown for a girl turning sixteen. It wasn't so much that I wanted it but rather an anticipated celebration that I was preened for from a very young age. My mother deemed it more necessary than I ever did, and she seemed to be making herself crazy with arranging the ideal location and the perfect dress for me to wear, but it irritated her that I didn't share in her overrated enthusiasm.

"I don't want this whole thing," I insisted while she took measurements of my chest and waist.

"Of course you do," she replied as if I had no opinion about it.

"Ma, please, we don't have to do all of this."

"Turn around," she commanded. "You're having the party, Francesca," she confirmed and with her hands on her hips and disgust in her eyes, she added. "Why can't you ever be normal?" Normal, to her, meant that I was supposed to conform to what all of the other girls my age were. She wanted the giggly, boy-crazy daughter who would work in her Italian restaurant and go shopping with her on weekends, the one who spent hours primping in the mirror with her makeup and experimental hairstyles. She wanted to take me to the beauty parlor like the other mothers did with their daughters.

"I'm not like other girls," I reminded her, just as I had a thousand times before. In reality, I was a tomboy who didn't even have many female friends, the disease rendered by of my tough girl persona, and it irritated my mother. She didn't know what to make of my behavior, and I think part of her suspected that I was a lesbian, too.

"Do what your mother says," my father intervened as he entered the kitchen, hardly even aware of the subject, and I saw a grin of triumph cross her face.

"Can't we just have a small party at the restaurant or something?" I pleaded.

"No!" My mother snapped and I hung my head.

"Carmella, miele, she doesn't want this thing," my father said in a sudden understanding of my feelings. "We'll just have a small thing at the restaurant." Like most Sicilians, "thing" seemed to be my father's favorite word.

It was clear by the pained expression on my mother's face that she was disappointed with his decision, especially after years of anxious planning for the occasion but, as I said before, no one was courageous enough to argue with my father.

"You're still wearing a nice dress and getting your hair done," she demanded, using the opportunity to finally get what she wanted. "You're going to look like a lady in the pictures." It was just like my mother to concern herself with outward appearances rather than my feelings.

Chapter 2

The restaurant was overflowing with Uncle Leo, Angelo, Carmine and the rest of our crew for my birthday celebration, and each one who walked through the door carried in an envelope filled with money, five hundred lira here, one thousand there. It's just what was given within our clan on special occasions. We took care of each other.

"Francesca, miele, I've never seen you look more beautiful," Uncle Carmine's blond haired wife, Sophia, who wreaked of makeup and perfume remarked.

"That dress is fantiastico," Lucia, Uncle Leo's wife, who always dyed her hair jet black, complimented.

"Isn't she aggettivo?" My mother responded to them before I even got the opportunity to say thank you. I felt dreadful in the blue flowered dress that she had chosen for me, but I couldn't deny that my long brown curls swept gently up looked pretty good. It was certainly the most feminine I had felt in quite some time, but it felt strange and uncomfortable to be in a dress.

"I look just like a high-priced hooker," I responded to my mother's obvious embarrassment. "I could bring in some good money downtown."

Toward the end of the party, Uncle Gino approached. "Your father told me about your little business venture," he commented with a grin. "Not bad, kid. Maybe after college, you could do a little work with us." Both of us giggled at his ribbing as he patted me on the shoulder, but it was common knowledge that women truly weren't welcomed in their line of business.

"Well, who needs college dressed like this, eh?" I ribbed.

By this time, it was really no secret to me that they were the Cosa Nostra, the Sicilian Mafia, though no one dared confirm my assumption. Still, the older I grew, the more obvious it became. I had seen enough gangster movies and overheard enough of their conversations to know what they were without seeing them in action. My father was the capo, Lorenzo Mazonelli, and nearly the entire town answered to him. He was the boss of all bosses, as well as a member of the Commission, and when he spoke, everyone listened closely to his words. He was the most respected and powerful man around. He had formed prominent relationships with police officers, judges, even politicians, and he was graciously welcomed everywhere that he went. To me, his life was a mysterious glory, the intriguing world of money, status, power and respect. I craved it all and I wanted in. Gino's words sang loudly in my ears but it all felt like a pipe dream.

With the money that I had earned from my own business, I bought a little beater of a car that was in good condition, but it needed some cosmetic work before it would be what I wanted. I seized the opportunity to use this excuse as a way into the "business".

"No, I'm not giving you a job in the garage," my father responded when I asked for some part-time work. "Women don't belong there. I will get the work done on the car and you will work in your mother's restaurant like a young signora should."

The last thing that I wanted was to be stuck in the kitchen of the restaurant, cooking food and washing dishes. Owning the restaurant was my mother's dream but, to me, it was merely a minimum wage job that I knew would take me nowhere and, frankly, I was making more money in my own business dealings. I needed a challenge that would jumpstart success. I was bred for a career of power and respect, one that would ensure my financial freedom, but my father had spoken and his decision was final. The restaurant would have to suffice, at least for the time being.

After a few weeks of laboring in the kitchen, my mother elevated me to a waitress, which enabled tips, and I did pretty well considering that most of the customers were Mafiosi who knew and took care of me. I also discovered, probably for the first time in my life, that I was attractive to men, and I quickly learned to use it to my advantage. My flirtatious smiles and conversation with them earned me a lot of money and many of them became repeat customers, stopping in almost daily to see me. That's how I met Marco.

I was instantly attracted to him, his bronzed, muscular physique and strong jaw line, dark hair and vivid green eyes that I felt analyzing me up and down as I approached his table. He was of strong Sicilian descent.

"What's your name?" He probed with a deep voice and the sexiest smile that I had ever seen, one that sent shivers through me and captured my breath, all at the same time. I was surprised that he didn't already know who I was since most knew me as the capo's daughter.

"Francesca," I replied softly with the most appealing grin and femininity that I could muster as his stare pulsated my stomach.

"You are truly gorgeous with those beautiful brown eyes," the handsome stranger smoothly complimented and, whether it was sincere or not, I was savoring every second of it. "You must hear that all the time."

My face burned with a timid smile as I found myself deficient of words, and my tingling stomach awakened parts of me that I had never before acknowledged. I felt as if my racing heart would pound its way right out of my chest amid the struggle to breathe in his presence. I refused to do anything that might push him away. This stranger invoked an array of unfamiliar, passionate emotions at the brink of spewing from deep within me. I had been caught off guard, entirely ill-equipped for my next action. The usual men that frequented the restaurant were harmless, non-intimidating, unattractive, easy targets to manipulate but Marco was of a different breed, distinctive and exceptional in his presence. I was frozen with intrigue, powerlessly captivated by his very being.

"Can I buy you dinner sometime, Francesca?" He asked, and I adored the sound of my name flowing from his inviting lips.

"Be calm," I silently reminded myself. No man, other than my father, that is, had weakened me like this man did. "Treat him like you do all the others," I told myself and, with that, I gathered my confidence and slipped him my number with a flirtatious grin before suavely strutting away from the table. I made my escape to the bathroom, jubilantly jumping up and down like the typical schoolgirl that I had always loathed until the door suddenly opened. He walked in with debonair assurance as my eyes widened with astonishment. Gently, he backed me against the wall with his hand on my cheek and kissed me, uncontrollably, with his velvet lips. My thrilled heart was racing with pleasure from his aggression, the mutual hunger between us kidnapping my judgment. He lifted his mouth from mine and stared, attentively, into my eyes.

"I couldn't help myself," he said with a grin in his perfect male tone as my eyes welcomed him for more. Marco lowered his soft lips back to mine, his passionate kiss sparking an erotic flame inside of me. "Meet me for dinner tonight," he requested, and I was ecstatic to oblige him.

"Francesca," my mother interrupted with a knock on the door, "are you in there?"

"Yes, Ma, I'll be right out," I called to her, nervously clearing my throat before moving in for one last kiss from my handsome stranger.

I overflowed with excitement at the thought of seeing Marco again, and our dinner date seemed like it would never arrive. In my new red dress, long, curled hair and makeup done flawlessly, I felt like a goddess and almost looked like one, too. A final gaze in the full-length mirror assured me that I looked beautiful, like a woman of sophistication, no longer the tough guy inside.

"Wow!" My mother exclaimed at the sight of my newfound femininity. Her tomboy of a daughter had been transformed into a lady. "Look at you. You're so gorgeous."

"Thanks, Ma, I won't be late," I told her, attempting a quick exit.

"Whoa, isn't this boy coming to pick you up and meet me like a gentleman should?" I should have known it was coming.

"No, I told him I'd just meet him back at the brothel," I joked but she didn't find it at all funny. "Since I don't know him very well, I feel more comfortable just meeting him at the restaurant." I had fabricated the truth because, though I didn't know Marco's age, I was sure that he was several years older than me, which my parents would never have approved of. I played it safe by telling my mother that it was a boy from school and, though she didn't know him, it somehow made her more at ease.

At the restaurant, my handsome date stood to greet me in a navy blue suit, his dark hair gelled to a slight wet look and the smile that I had fallen immediately in love with. He looked distinguished and gentlemanly, and it took my breath away to see that out of every other woman in the establishment, he was waiting for me.

"Wow, you look so amazing," he complimented with a kiss of my hand and the aroma of his cologne tempted me to take him right there where we stood.

"Oh, well thank you," I replied as he pulled out my chair. His chivalry made him seem too good to be true. It was something that I would have never gotten from a boy my age and I was exceedingly impressed.

Staring at me from across the table, he took my hands in his. "I couldn't wait to see you again," he spoke softly in his baritone, Italian accent. "I knew, as soon as I saw you, I just had to make you mine, no matter what it takes." His words were compelling and provocative poetry in my ears, piquing my senses to a height they had never before seen. His gaze refused to release mine as we sat in a breathless world of our own, where no one else existed at all. Racing through me were unfamiliar emotions of passion that overwhelmed my entire body. Never had I wanted so desperately for a man to touch me, to ravish me into womanhood. I hadn't yet felt the affectionate caress of a boy, nor had I ever craved it up until that moment, when it was all that I wanted. "I've never met a woman like you," Marco said and his words dragged me from the fantasy dancing in my head. I wasn't a woman but a child, an adolescent girl who only appeared a woman. He needed to know but I couldn't find the affirmation. The words would force him immediately away from me, and I knew that I couldn't bear to lose him. At some point, he would need to know that I was only sixteen but I decided that it wouldn't be that night.

"I've never met a man like you," was my response to his compliment, and it was true. He was distinguished and charming with a flair of enthralling aggression for what he wanted. He was powerful persuasion and irresistible bliss, and I was utterly smitten with him.

Marco spared no expense as we dined over filet minion, lobster and the most expensive of white wine, and it became obvious to me that he preferred the finer things in life, one of which, in his eyes, was me. I played the part, the role of a slightly older, sophisticated and confident woman whose affection he needed to earn, and he seemed to fall all over himself trying to do just that. It was then that I saw the power that women truly had over men, and the magnetism of it all thrilled me inside and out.

"I love an independent woman with a hint of attitude," he told me in adoration of my personality, "like you, playing hard to get." His grin was that of amusement. I hoped that I was invigorating him that way that he excited me.

"Well," I flashed a confident smile, "the best things in life are well worth the hard work, don't you think?"

"Most definitely," he agreed with a grin, seemingly loving every minute of my cat and mouse ploy.

I had to admit that the game was highly arousing to me, as

well. It was a turn-on to possess the control that I had over him and give him only a small taste of something he craved. The chase was electrifying to both of us.

We danced slowly, erotically to the soft piano music in the background, each of us hungry for the other's touch, yet neither greedy to acquire it. Marco's embrace lent security, the delightful aroma of his cologne invigorating my senses. God, how I wanted that man. My need for him only escalated by the second, and I wasn't sure how much longer I could hold out. But it had now become a competition of a sort to see which of us gave in first, and I was determined not to lose.

"You are truly sorprendente, Francesca," he softly whispered in my ear, sending a shiver through my very soul.

His satin lips lightly caressed their way down my neck, arousing every sensual emotion within me and, when he found his way to my lips, I moaned with ecstasy. His tongue danced in gentle glee with mine, igniting hunger that I had never felt before until it evolved into an explosive yearning for him. The passion between us had become unimaginable, and I felt as if I would die without his touch.

"What do you say we get outta here," Marco softly suggested, and I knew his intentions. I desperately wanted to leave with him, to be alone in our intensifying ardor. I ached for his hands on me, and it was he that I yearned to discover my womanhood with. Never had I fathomed such a quick surrender of myself to a man until that moment. It didn't matter that I hardly knew him or that I was of such a tender age. It didn't even matter to me that I had never before experienced a man. My rationale had been long misplaced and all that mattered that night was being with him.

The two of us could hardly contain our shameless actions to Marco's Cadillac, in the parking lot, and I hoped that our destination was nearby.

"My house is miles from here and I can't wait that long," he huffed in between his ravaged kisses. "Where's your place?" Since I still lived with my parents, my house was not an option.

"I can't wait that long," I moaned, and we decided on a hotel down the block.

He opened the door and squeezed his body to mine against the wall, kissing me uncontrollably, and it drove me wild.

"I need you so badly," he whispered, hiking up my mini skirt and lifting my leg to his hip, and as much as I craved him, too, I refused to let my first sexual experience be a quickie against the wall. We were so much into one another that I hadn't even noticed what the room looked like.

"Whoa, hold on," I stopped him, staring into his eyes. "I'd like it to last for a while." I couldn't bring myself to admit that I was a virgin, though I was sure he would know afterward anyway.

He peered back at me, seemingly dumbstruck. "You're right, I'm sorry. Let's have a drink and enjoy our time together."

The room of the swanky hotel housed a king sized bed and fully equipped bar with a pair of white, fluffy robes and a jacuzzi tub. After a glass of wine and some light conversation, I sat on the silky comforter of the bed in eager anticipation of him. His kisses became slow and passionate as he gently undressed me, softly exploring every inch of my skin with his fingers and lips, and my body tingled with exhilaration as it pleaded for more. I screamed out with pleasure as quivering waves of ecstasy hijacked my muscles, but he had just gotten started. He moved slowly and passionately on top of me, his soft skin warming mine while he hands traced my body until we blissfully climaxed together. The experience was the most erotic moment of my life.

As he lay, holding me in the security of his arms, it became clear that he knew my secret when his question was asked. "Were you a . . . um . . . was that your first time?" My face stung with embarrassment but I recovered my tough girl persona.

"So what if I am? You got a problem with that?"

"Hey, calm down," my lover softly giggled with a kiss on my cheek. Slowly, he guided my bashful eyes to his. "I think it's incredible," he whispered and bestowed more of his passion upon me. That night, Marco brought the woman out in me over and over again, and I swore that it was the best night of my life. I wished that my heaven would never find its end.

Chapter 3

Marco was stopping in at my mother's restaurant every week to see me, and we stole every chance that we had to make love. We frequented upscale hotels, fields, his car, anywhere that we could be alone for our impassioned endeavors, and he made me feel like the sexiest woman alive. He was still not aware of my young age, and it was obvious that he didn't know that Lorenzo Mazonelli was my father. I was certain that our relationship would end abruptly if he did. No boy was brazen enough to try dating the mob boss's daughter. Eventually, I would have to reveal my secrets to my lover but I couldn't bring myself to confess just yet. Our relationship was kept a secret from my parents and Marco never disputed my decision to do so. He was twenty-eight years old and he believed that I was nineteen, still a bit young for him but an adult just the same.

"Why don't we ever go to your house?" I asked him during one of our rendezvous.

"I have a roommate so there's no privacy," he told me and, though I found it a little peculiar, I chose to accept the situation for what it was, perhaps more so in an effort to thwart off any probing of my own home life.

We talked about our lives, from our childhood to the present, our goals and ambitions, family and relationships. I told him of my father's success in business and my desire to follow in his footsteps.

"I don't want to run that restaurant," I said. "I need a challenge."

"How about working for me?" He probed with sly eyebrows. I had never even asked what he did for a living, yet my intrigue was undeniable. He appeared to be a success at whatever it was that he did, and I would have done almost anything to escape the suffocating walls of my mother's restaurant.

"What would I be doing?" It didn't really matter because I was ready for a change. I probably would have scrubbed toilets just to earn my freedom.

Marco explained that he was a loan officer of a sort and said all I had to do is collect the payments, each month, from specific business owners in the area. It sounded pretty simple to me and I was eager to begin my journey of independence.

My parents weren't exactly thrilled with the idea of me quitting the restaurant and I'm sure much of it had to do with my mother's inability to observe my activities. The interrogation soon followed.

"What kind of job is this?" My infuriated mother probed.

"What will you be doing?" My father added suspiciously.

"What is so wrong with the restaurant? You will own it one day," my mother again intervened, clearly agitated by my decision.

My responses were subtle and short, as little as I could get away with in order to satisfy their anxiety. The less they knew, the better, I felt. The last thing I wanted was them prying into my blossoming relationship with Marco, and I certainly wasn't willing to be treated like a child any longer, even if I still was one. My father knew nearly everyone in town and chances were that he knew Marco too, or knew of him, at least. I refused to have him spy on us and ruin what we were building, nor did I want him to find out that my new boyfriend was twelve years my senior. There were aspects of my life that were just better left unknown to others.

The work at my new job came easy for me. I made my rounds to the various businesses on my list, collecting their monthly payments for Marco, and I got a percentage, a commission of a sort, for my success. Not only was I making good money right from the beginning, but every business that I went to had the payment ready for me to pick up. It couldn't have been any easier and, for me, it was working out perfectly.

Marco and I continued our rendezvous but I had to admit that our frequent stays in various hotel rooms, even the more lavish ones, were growing old, quickly. I wanted to experience his world, his life, but always, he had an excuse.

"Are you married?" I finally asked him, almost certain that I already knew the answer. "I mean, we never go to your house and I'm thinking that it's because you have a wife there."

"You're crazy, ragazza," he responded with a ridiculous snicker. "I don't have a wife but I do have a tiny little two-room bachelor pad that's too small and messy to take you to, not to mention my nosy roommate. That's all it is, babe." He caressed my cheek with his satin fingers, staring sincerely into my eyes. "I wouldn't do that to you. You know me." His alluring eyes and voice of promise were all it ever took to halt my suspicions. All I ever needed was to feel that he was mine.

"How about we get you a new apartment?" He suggested, and I was certain that it was the solution for halting my questions about his life. Freedom was an enticing idea but I knew that my parents would never agree. There was no way that they would permit me to live alone at sixteen years old.

"Um, well, I don't want to leave my roommate on her own," was my excuse. "I don't think she could make the rent by herself. Besides, she does all the cooking." I despised lying to Marco and swore that I would surely get it back in karma, but I couldn't let him know the truth.

"Are you her mother?" He smirked. We both laughed off his comment. "Listen, on a serious note, I have something for you," he added. From a white cloth, Marco revealed a .45 caliber gun. I still remember the stunned glare that must have overtaken my face when I saw his offering. Even with my father being who he was, I had never been around guns and the thought of carrying one left me apprehensive.

"Do I really need this?" I asked him. My work, up to that point, had never warranted it.

"Listen, when it comes to money, you can never be too careful," he casually replied. "You might never need it but, in case you ever do, you have to be secure with it."

Marco drove me out to a remote field, where he spread out a blanket and picnic lunch, complete with flowers. We sat near a small stream that trickled through the grass, eating a light lunch and sipping wine.

"You are one amazing guy," I remarked, captivated by his appeal.

"I'm just a peasant behind a flawless queen," he responded, kissing me with a swelling passion. "I can't live without you, Francesca. I love you and I always want you to be mine."

I wanted it, too. The thought of being cradled in his arms every night and waking with him beside of me each morning was my dream. Marco was everything I felt a man should be, and I had very clear visions of a life together as husband and wife.

He grabbed the empty wine bottle and walked several feet away from me. "See if you can hit this," he yelled out to me, positioning the bottle on a log.

I grabbed the gun and warily rose to my feet with trembling hands as Marco made his way back to me. The weight felt foreign in my grip as my palms sweated around it. I struggled to find a steadiness as I aimed at my target.

"Wait a minute," Marco intervened. "Just hold and familiarize yourself with the gun first. Make sure you're comfortable with it. It has to be an extension of you."

I listened, carefully, to his instructions, acquainting myself with the cold steel.

"It's an extension of your hand," Marco coached. "It belongs there. It's comodo there." His words calmed my anxiety until I slowly lifted the gun with a steady hand and one eye closed, the bottle in my sights. With a deep breath, I pulled the trigger. *Crash!*

"You hit it!" Marco proudly exclaimed. "What a shot!" I flashed a proud grin, anxious for more. The power in my hands propelled me into an immediate addiction. It was an aphrodisiac to possess such control, and each shot seemed to empower me.

My newfound strength thrilled me with its superiority and I realized a place in me that I never knew existed. The power I possessed permitted me aggression and control that was exerted, even in our intimate moments, an uninhibited freedom that Marco had only assumed absent in me. I was his delicate daisy who had suddenly blossomed into an exotic vine, challenging his submission. The strong steel of the gun demanded his trust in me as its coldness claimed his throat when we made love that day. It turned him on to have my weapon pointed at his jugular, rendering him uncertain of my intentions while still submitting to him the ultimate role-playing fantasy, an untamed game of erotica.

Marco and I spent most of the day target shooting, sipping wine and making love. I had discovered my true passion for guns, my natural ability and comfort with shooting. It wasn't long before I added a couple more to my arsenal for my newfound hobby.

It soon became that I was rarely at home with my parents, other than to sleep and go to school. I spent all of my afternoons and evenings working with Marco and target shooting but, just as I had expected, my parents began probing my steady absence and acquaintances.

"I don't know any of your friends anymore," my mother ranted. "Who are you spending your time with?"

"I'm . . ."

"You're never home."

"Ma, I . . ." I struggled to answer as her Sicilian-laced interrogation continued.

"Ah me, are you on drugs?"

"Why, did you find my pipa? Ma, stop it!" I rebutted, to her surprise. "You're making me pazzo! I'm not using drugs, I'm not an alcoholic and I'm not out stealing or killing. I'm working and that's all," I insisted with the hope of silencing her.

"You stay out of the dark world!" She firmly demanded.

The dark world. To my mother, it was my father's world, the Cosa Nostra. It was the life that my father had chosen for us, one that she could never fight as a subservient Sicilian wife and, though our family delighted in the luxuries of my father's elite status, the criminal aspect of it was never something that she condoned. She was a devout Catholic, torn between Christianity and loyalty to her husband in the days when there were simply no choices for women. My mother had always done her best to shelter me from my father's world, and it was her fear that I would marry into it as well.

"You will get an education and marry a doctor", she continuously preached. We had seen my father through several stints in prison and many nights of hiding out from the authorities, a life of hardship and loneliness where my mother was forced to pick up the pieces and, often times, figure things out on her own. I recalled many nights of traveling in night hours to go visit him so that we weren't noticed or followed to his secret locations. I spent many years of my childhood visiting him in prisons, where I sat with him and my mother at a lifeless, steel table in ordinary conversation about school or home. None were ever personal and all were short lived. I noticed my mother's weary eyes and forced smile as she suffered the consequences of his behavior, the way that she courageously picked up where he left off, when everyone else seemed to have disappeared.

I listened closely to her words but my obsession with the Cosa Nostra couldn't be ignored. I craved the power that was my father's, the respect that he was granted. I had spent years romanticizing his success but the mere idea of a female Mafiosi was unheard of. Those were the days that women spent their lives cooking, cleaning and raising their children while the men did as they pleased. A woman could never be permitted into a man's business world.

I had spent my entire life obeying my father, fully

submissive to his every command, as my mother had. His choices were ours, as well, and our voices were rarely heard. I refused to become my mother. My life would be different. I would carry the power that I was never permitted at the hands of my father. For me, life would be better. I would live it my way and reap my own rewards rather than depending on a man as most women did.

By the time I turned seventeen, my hobby had made me a sharp-shooter. Seven guns made up my arsenal and I could handle each one like an expert. It was an adrenalin rush that nothing else could provide. The cold steel was my confidence, my power. I kept them well hidden in the new car I had recently bought for fear of my parents discovering them.

My high school graduation rapidly approached, which threw my mother into a tailspin, planning another gala that she craved more than I did. As always, the ever loyal members of my mafia family arrived with envelopes of lira and their congratulations.

"What is the new graduate going to do next?" Uncle Carmine inquired.

"Well, I . . ."

"She's going to istituto," my mother intervened before I could respond.

"Ma, please!" I yelled with agitation. "I'm not going to college!" There it was. I had blurted disappointment at her in a blatant embarrassment of the worst kind. My words seemed to catapult her into a state of shock, and the expression on her face was as if she'd just been shot or perhaps stricken with a fatal diagnosis. I could see her gathering her words that would soon be spewed at me.

"What, you want to be a casalinga with no goals of your own? You want to be a scadente on the street?" She began ranting with the frantic gestures of her hands that always accompanied her lectures, and I found it amusing that the woman whose goal had always been preparing me as a housewife now found such importance in independence. "You're going to get an education!"

"Ma, can we just talk about this later?" I pleaded. My

graduation party was the last place that I wanted to be scolded by my mother.

"Yes, we're going to talk about it," she replied before stomping off, irritably.

When the party ended, I had a cool ten thousand lira, plenty of cash for an apartment of my own. It was time to fly and I couldn't have been more ready. My parents had a difference of opinion, of course.

"You're not old enough to move out," my father growled.

"That's right, and you're going to college," my mother added. I felt like I might as well have been talking to a wall when it came to reasoning with them. In our house, my voice was mute and my opinions were void but my determination never waned.

"Ma, I told you, I'm not going to college." Her sudden enthusiasm about me getting a higher education was baffling.

"You're going to make something out of your life," my father sternly demanded.

"Oh, you mean like you did?" My sarcastic truth was a pill, enormous and jagged to swallow, that left him stunned and speechless, probably for the first time ever, and I was proud of my courageous rebuttal. Even more surprising was my mother's silence, awkwardly piercing the room.

"Francesca, you are not using your graduation money for an appartamento," my bullying father barked.

"That money belongs to me to use as I wish," I argued with a fearless face. "But since I have a job, which you've both seem to have forgotten, I don't need to use it." The walls of my parents' house were suffocating me and I was determined to move out, in spite of their feelings about it. It was time to begin a life of my own.

After only a short search, I leased a spacious luxury villa amid vibrant tropical gardens and multihued stone walkways. Spectacular brick archways accented every entrance amid gleaming ceramic floors. Magnificent chandeliers dazzled, gracefully, above the gorgeous, hand-crafted fireplace in the sitting room while an ornamental iron rail trailed the stairs to three small bedrooms, each with its own terrace. I was awestruck by the ocean view from the private, stone floored patio running the length of the villa.

"This is incredible," I told myself, still numb to the reality of it being my new home.

At last, I could savor the taste of freedom. I was an adult, living my own life in a spectacular world that I had created. No longer was I pressed beneath the harsh thumb of my father. I was living the ultimate dream and for a seventeen year old girl and my Eden was sheer euphoria.

Chapter 4

I sat confidently in my new, designer pants suit, silently poised with my legs crossed, in Marco's office, awaiting his return.

"Come stai, Francesca?" A dark-eyed, handsome associate in the office greeted. His name was Georgio Armisi and I had met him only a few times prior. "Waiting for Marco?" I had never witnessed him without his usual polite smile but, that day, it yielded ulterior motives.

"I am," I answered kindly. "He told me that he's on his way." A nervous tremble invaded me when he approached to sit next to me.

"While we're waiting, I have a business proposition for you," he uttered. Maybe I should have ignored his words but I couldn't deny my intrigue. "How do you feel about flying?"

A week later, on Tuesday morning, I nervously prepared for my covert excursion to Madrid, Spain. All I had to do, Georgio explained, was discreetly deliver five kilos of cocaine, a swift exchange that would still lend plenty of time for shopping and sightseeing, during my two-day stay. I understood the risks involved, being caught and imprisoned or even being killed. My decision wasn't about money. I already had money. The challenge was my driving force. The quest fed my hunger for danger. Succeeding in the mission would only further prove my strength.

With a deep breath, I peered at my reflection in the full-length mirror, envisioning my mother's shame. What I was about to do would never be condemned by her but, for me, it was merely part of the plan – money, power, control and most of all, respect.

Georgio had strategically implanted the drugs in the bottom of an altered suitcase and I was ready for my trip. The walk to check my luggage catapulted me into turbulence as the realty of my crime set in. Maintaining a sophisticated calm above my shaky hands and beads of sweat was a growing challenge. The rising voltage in the pit of my stomach electrified my nausea until my rush to oust it.

"Toughen up, you've got this," I reassured myself in the small restroom mirror and, with a cleansing breath, I made my way through airport security.

Relief rushed through me as I took my seat on the plane. I had only one more security point to get through in Madrid. It was an alien destination, full of the unknown, and I had only a few simple instructions to guide me through it. I would be doing business with a stranger who had the potential to subject me to his own control, a power that could render me a victim of any circumstance, but Georgio had assured my safety and the simplicity of my mission.

"I have people who do this for me all the time," he had told me. "Airport security is minimum and customs agents won't suspect a professional looking woman like you." It hadn't taken much to convince me.

After several hours, the airport reenergized my nerves and the nausea returned with ferocity. I had been abandoned in a world of the unfamiliar with only myself and more trepidation than I had ever known, but the echo of Georgio's words in my ear fed my confidence.

Squeaking through the dubious eyes of airport security seemed a breeze compared to what I faced beyond it. A taxi escorted me to a petite, dilapidated motel on a darkened side street.

"Are you sure this is the place?" I asked the driver and, with his nod of assurance, I checked into my room where I was to wait for my new business partner's phone call.

I sat in the filthy suffocation of the small hole by the tiny black and white television's glow with the realization that I was not on the vacation that I had been promised. The walls could have orated a hundred horror stories of its victims. Hours felt like weeks inside of the barren, pale walls that I was forbidden to abandon. I sat tautly, drenched from the heat, though the room felt cold. The monotony and realization of my circumstances invoked panic as I plotted my escape. I wouldn't linger another day in the closet-like prison. If my contact didn't call that night, I would go to him, I decided.

The piercing ring of the telephone frightened me from a snooze, though I couldn't recall falling asleep.

"You alone?" The deep voice asked in broken English.

"Of course," I responded, wondering why anyone else would have even wanted to be in a place like that and, within seconds, he was knocking on the door.

He was a muscular, dark-haired man with a bushy beard and menacing eyes that guardedly scanned the room and then me. I replaced my frightful glare with an audacious face in an attempt to rebuke his intimidation.

"Where is it?" He probed and I motioned to my suitcase. I watched as he sifted through its contents before dumping everything on the floor.

"Hey!" I intervened, rushing to retrieve my belongings and, with one long stride, the beast was before me with a firm grip on my throat.

"Where is it?" He repeated, intensely, reducing me to a mere mouse as he pinned me against the wall. My breath slowly began to fade.

"Inside," was all that I could manage in his grasp. I could feel the absence of air slow my heart and I felt like I would lose consciousness.

"Show me," the man demanded, releasing me. I felt the tiny room spinning and regaining its dull hue as I revealed what he'd been searching for. I eagerly awaited the approval that never showed in him.

The stranger stabbed through the tape with a small pocket knife to sample the goods while my goal was to get the money and run quickly out of there.

"I have a plane to catch so can we finish this up?" I uttered in my tough girl demeanor while my heart pounded at the thought of him killing me right there, which could've been very easily accomplished and probably without anyone even knowing for days. With his callous stare, he relinquished the money and I have to admit that I didn't even count it. As soon as he exited the room, so did I, as quickly as I could.

The airport never looked so appealing but I was forced to wait three days to fly back so as to dull any suspicions. Refusing to remain where I was, I found another hotel nearby, in a brighter and seemingly safer part of town, where crimson and yellow buildings lined cobblestone streets.

The petite hotel room felt like luxury after the hole I had just escaped with its generous bedding, clean carpet and sanitary bathroom. I was finally able to relax and, in the days that followed, I behaved like a tourist on vacation, swimming in the hotel pool and shopping at the vibrantly colored, local shops. I successfully returned to Sicily to find Georgio awaiting me.

"How was the trip?" He greeted with his friendly smile.

"Oh, grande," I replied, sarcastically, "except that you forgot to mention the ratty motel and that my contact is a complete maniac!"

"It's a drug deal, sweetheart," he responded nonchalantly. "Did you expect to see the Pope?"

"Forget it." I was too exhausted to argue.

"You got the money?" He probed lightheartedly.

"Yes." I couldn't bask in his enthusiasm. I was angry and worn, and all I wanted was to go home.

"Well, smile," he said. "You just made a lot of money." At

that point, I didn't care about anything but my sanctuary.

I had led Marco to believe only that my excursion was a family trip, and Georgio and I had kept it our secret. That evening, I called Marco to tell him that I was home and a woman answered.

"I'm sorry, I must have the wrong number," I uttered softly. "I'm looking for Marco."

"I'm his wife," she rigidly informed me. "Who is this?" I sat in a dumbfounded silence that the man I loved, the man I had planned to marry, already had a wife and I felt foolish for not recognizing the signs that had already warned of it. "Let me guess," she added. "You're the new flavor of the month." My heart fell to my stomach as I let out a silent gasp. "There are a hundred others like you, miele, but let me tell you that he will always be with me," and with that, she hung up.

I couldn't believe what I had just heard. The only man that I had ever loved had completely betrayed me, and I needed to hear it from him. How could he truly love me and be married to someone else? I wondered. He had declared himself mine and I felt that he was. To me, it was she who was the other woman, as if our roles were reversed. It felt like the breath had just been beaten out of me. I suffocated at my image of her with Marco and I needed to find him. I had to talk to him and force him to see my agony. I needed to know why he had lied to me and, moreover, I demanded to know which of us he truly loved. Who had his future? My mind was reeling with images of Marco with other women and it was them, even more than his wife, who threatened my security. Too infuriated to cry or even sit still, I paced the floor of my living room, impatiently searching my mind for the words that I would discharge at my lover. A woman scorned, I was rapidly losing control and it increased with each minute that I didn't hear from him.

Alcohol became my remedy, a gradual numbing of the insult that I had been tossed. I found myself drowning those flaring images of his women that seared my eyes until my vision was blurred enough to sleep.

The morning jarred me with the constant buzz of the

doorbell. My head thumped while my stomach threatened to expel its poison, and the struggle to pull myself out of bed was agonizing. Daylight scorched my eyes as I sluggishly stumbled to the door.

Marco stood, handsomely clad as always, in his gray suit and tie. The aroma of his cologne that usually intoxicated me was suddenly nauseating. All of the grief that I felt the night before rushed in with a vengeance when I saw his adoring green eyes.

I left him at the open door to retrieve the aspirin and returned to suspicion glaring at my new personality, the one that he had never seen before.

"How was your trip?" He asked as if nothing had changed between us.

"Oh, fine, and how's your wife?" I responded with swollen eyes and elevated eyebrows.

Marco peered at me in silence, unsure of his next move. He had been busted and his attempt to squirm out of the situation was obvious.

"Francesca, I'm sorry," he began. "I wanted to tell you but I was afraid of losing you." He knelt down and took my hand in his. "Please, forgive me. I love you." He arose to sit on the couch next to me. "Listen, it's complicated with Ava. Our marriage hasn't been good for a long time, but the truth is that she's unstable and on medication for depression and bipolar disorder. A divorce would be devastating to her, mentally and, though I'm not happy, I'm also not willing to further compromise her health. I'm sorry. I should have told you instead of you finding out this way."

I had always sworn that I wouldn't be any man's fool but I couldn't deny falling victim to his story. My anger shifted to sympathy for him, even applauding him for struggling to resurrect his loveless marriage and sparing her feelings. Besides, I thought, how could I really fault him for his lies when I had a few of my own?

"How many others are there, besides me?" I probed.

"I have actually dated a few before you but they were flings, niente. Francesca, I really fell for you. You make me feel something that no one ever has before. You are everything that I always wanted. I see my future in you and I hope that you'll let me love you forever."

It was that moment that transformed me into precisely the woman I had always loathed, the fragile one who was content being a mistress rather than the wife. Perhaps it was my underlying need for Marco that had overpowered my sensibility but, whatever the reason, I forgave him, and hearing that he still loved me somehow perfected my world again.

"Let me put you back in bed so you can rest," he said and as he lay in the covers, cradling me in his comfort, I rewarded myself with his velvet lips on mine in a soft and passionate unity that stole my breath while leaving me starved for more. His kiss, alone, ignited a hunger in me that only he could invoke. At that moment, I yearned for him more than anything else in the world, desperate to make time stand still so that he would, forever, belong to me.

"I need you so much," I softly pleaded as he pulled me tightly to him, making me his own, his velvet caress on my skin with the warmth of him against me. I craved him like no other, and his touch was my nourishment. We swayed, slowly together, our bodies fused as one, and I felt as if I couldn't get close enough but I had his entirety. He was a drug, my poisoned pleasure, lending to my addiction only enough for my survival.

"God, I love you," he uttered into my eyes, bringing us both to an erotic eruption of ecstasy.

Later, as we lay, comfortably weary-eyed, on the verge of a nap, Marco kissed my forehead.

"I meant what I said to you, Francesca. I really do love you," he spoke, softly, and I believed him. "There's just something about you that takes my breath away. You're different, strong and confident, independent and brave but even more is that you make me want to be a better man. You are the one, my soul mate, and seeing you with another man would suffocate me."

"You're the only man I'll ever want," I assured him. It was true, I had never loved anyone the way that I loved him, and I vowed to love him forever.

Chapter 5

The thousands that I had gained from my trip convinced me to take a second one. Even with the impending risk, it was the easiest money I had ever made and just a few more trips would leave me financially set for quite a while.

Georgio booked my flight to Munich for the following week. I insisted on a lodging upgrade and, though an upper class hotel was out of the question with all of its security, he did agree on nicer accommodations.

Neither Marco nor my parents knew the real reason behind my trip and I never felt it necessary to reveal it to them, but they weren't without questions.

"Where are you going on these trips?" My parents probed, as did Marco. I led him to believe that I was traveling with my family while they thought my excursions were business related. In a sense, they were.

Just as with my previous trip, my suitcase cloaked the drugs. I breezed through airport security and slept on the plane but, once again, my nerves got the best of me when we landed.

"You can do this," I convinced myself, wearily

approaching the stern-faced security officer. He peered suspiciously at me as I flashed a flirtatious grin to disguise my racing heart. One thing I had learned through the years was how being a young, attractive woman could benefit me, and this was a situation that I had to make it work.

"Your purse, please," he commanded in his native German tongue and I complied. "What brings you to Munich?" The inquisitive, middle-aged man queried while searching my belongings.

"Can't a girl have a little fun?" I replied with the seduction of a hungry lioness. I felt like I would pass out from the anxiety, and I hoped that he couldn't see the tense sweating that I felt flowing from my pores. He turned to write something and handed it to me as he waved me through. "Dinner?" it read with his telephone number and, with a snicker, I threw it away and headed to the hotel. I was to meet my contact at midnight.

The modest hotel was anything but lavish but it was clean and comfortable and, with the few hours that I had free, I treated myself to a quick swim in the pool and a nice dinner at a restaurant down the road. I wasn't sure how exactly I had expected Germany to look, but it reminded me of pictures I had always seen of London.

The knock came on the door at eleven o'clock, an hour early, and it made me edgy. He appeared through the window a harmless, almost meek man, clad in a dark blue suit.

"Francesca?" He asked nervously.

"Come in. You're early," I greeted.

"I wanted to get it done sooner." His bulging eyes were outlined with puffy, dark rings as he appeared to tremble in a profuse sweat. He seemed a bit shaky, which riled my nerves, and I needed him to calm down. "You got the stuff?" He questioned.

"If you've got the money," I answered.

"I want to test it first." He uncovered a syringe and spoon from the interior pocket of his jacket. I wasn't at all comfortable with the idea but, if it took that to get the deal done, then I wouldn't argue.

"Give me the money and you can try it while you're here," I insisted and he gave up the massive stack of bills.

I observed as he liquefied the cocaine on the spoon and heated it with a lighter before absorbing it into the syringe. Other than in the movies, it was the first time that I had ever seen it done in person. He tightened his belt around his arm, nearly cutting off the circulation, and struggled to locate a vein that was still intact from his years of penetrations. I counted the times that he stuck himself in both arms . . seven, eight, nine . . . before resorting to a vein in his neck and I felt sorry for him, inflicting so much on himself for a quick dose of his poison. He was unlike what I expected a drug dealer to be, an obvious veteran addict who, at that point, continued the drug for his survival rather than the mere enjoyment from which it began. With his head tilted back, he closed his eyes while the drug soaked his blood to numb his pain. It was a pathetic existence to me and I felt guilty for feeding his addiction.

"Gut," he commented in German, reaching for a second fix.

"Whoa, that's enough," I told him. "Time to move your party back to your house." He glared at me in a stunned silence as if I had four eyes. "Our deal here is done so it's time for you to go."

"Have some fun with me." He rose to his feet.

"No, I have a plane to catch," I replied but he looked too comfortable to leave, I suppose with the expectation of partying the night away with me.

"Come on," he uttered, pushing me to the bed. I felt the weight of him on top of me, his odor and foul breath in my nose, instantly repulsing me.

"Get off of me!" I demanded, fighting his busy hands that attempted to maul me.

"Don't refuse," the addict commanded in broken English, restraining my hands. My sudden knee to his groin forced him to the floor. I reached in the drawer of the night stand and pulled from it my comfort, my own addiction, and I aimed it at his chest.

"Now, since you can't play nice, here's your last warning,"

I told him. "Take that nasty stuff and get out right now!" The gun reiterated my demand, forcing him, quickly, out the door and I fell on the bed with relief, pondering if the money was really worth the trouble. Tears fell down my cheeks as I fought them. "Toughen up," I commanded myself. "Mobsters don't cry."

"I'm done with this", I told Georgio when I returned. "What kind of freaks are you dealing with?" I explained to him what had happened. "The money's not worth my life." Both trips had rendered horrible experiences.

"No, you're right, it's not and you handled yourself well out there," he responded. "These aren't church people, Francesca. The people you're meeting are hardcore criminals and drug dealers. You have to know what you're up against and, if you can't handle it, I can't send you anymore," he told me. "I'll go with you on the next one."

I headed for home in anticipation of a warm bath after such a disheartening trip, coupled with jet lag, but when I opened the door, my house was in shambles. Every room displayed overturned tables, tussled furniture and my valuables strewn across the floor. My bed looked as if it had been torched and the mirror on my dresser read *HE'S MINE!* in blood colored lipstick.

"Get over here now!" I yelled at Marco on the phone when I called. It was clear that the destruction was the handiwork of his wife who had, obviously, found his key.

Marco scanned the mess with bewildered eyes. "Are you sure this was her?" He asked until I showed him my bedroom mirror. He stared in disbelief. "I just can't imagine her doing this."

"Really, and why not?" I was infuriated at his notion of her innocence, as if he was protecting her rather than me, whom he had sworn to love most in the world. "She's bipolar, remember?"

He peered at me with guilt-stricken eyes. "Francesca, she is incinta."

"Pregnant?" The revelation shot through me with the force of a hundred cannons. Fury's heat slapped my face in his betrayal. Marco had sworn his love to me and promised forever, only to weave blatant lies into my head.

"I'm sorry, miele. I didn't mean for it to happen," he uttered softly.

"No, because you just fell into bed with her by accident, right?"

"She's my wife, Francesca."

"The same one that you've been trying to divorce?" The angry sarcasm was my only way of avoiding a breakdown. Marco was the only man that I had ever loved and I couldn't bear the thought of his arms around someone else, even his wife. I had, somehow, staked claim to him as mine.

"Francesca, please."

"Fuori", I sobbed and he approached to console me.

"Get out!" I screamed at him and, reluctantly, he walked out of my life as we wept.

His wife's loathing of me suddenly made sense, and I almost condoned what she had done to my house. Just as she had stolen the man I love, I had stolen hers. Both of us were left, tortured with heartbreak by the one man that each of us trusted. Perhaps I deserved what I had gotten. I left the disarray to sulk in the bathtub and the warmth of my bed.

The next morning, I was awakened by my parents ringing the doorbell.

"Coming," I called out while making my way through the obstacle course of my possessions. Distress invaded my mother's face when I opened the door.

"What happened?" She probed, analyzing the mess.

"Someone broke in while I was away," I answered. "It's okay, though, I have it under control."

"Who did this?" My father wanted to know, assumingly so that he could ensure traditional mafia punishment to whomever it was that had victimized me. A part of me wanted to tell him so that Marco got what I felt he deserved but a larger part of me would suffer to see him hurt.

"I don't know who did it, or why, Dad," I fibbed. "It was probably just a couple of baminos because hardly anything was taken. The sorrow I'd felt the previous night came rushing back with a sting to my eyes but I had to avoid the display at all costs. My father could never see weakness in my face because anything but strength was alien to him. For several hours, my parents helped me with the cleanup until my house returned to normal, and I was grateful, not only for their assistance but, moreover, for their company.

The following week brought the "family" to my house for dinner. They poured in, two by two – Gino, Anthony, Uncle Leo, Mario – each of them, my father's consiglieres, with bottles of wine and housewarming gifts. For us, three things were custom - loyalty, dinners and gifts. It was just the way of the Cosa Nostra. They were who everyone wanted as friends, yet feared the most. They either took care of you, controlled you or got rid of you so those who weren't "family" searched for ways to become an asset to them. Mafiosi were loan sharks, drug dealers, smugglers and extortionists who, for decades, had complete control of the town, right down to the police and even the Mayor. Their hands were on every business deal in town and they got a cut of everything. Money and respect were power and so was the mafia, in every sense of the word.

Though their activities were no secret, they were never discussed around the women. It had always been believed that only men belonged in the "family business" and the women had no place involved. We were only around at social gatherings, where food and family always seemed the topics of conversation.

The wives were famous for their gatherings of cooking and gossip but it was never for me. I was always more interested in the business aspects, even with being unwelcome there. I wanted the opportunity to prove myself, and the trips that I had taken were a great start. I was determined to make my mark in their world.

"Francesca, aren't you afraid to stay here, alone, after the break-in?" Caroline asked.

"Say the word and I'll handle the creep," Gino inserted.

"No, no, everything is fine, really," I insisted. "I can handle myself."

"I'll put a couple of guys outside at night," my father told me.

"No, Papa, grazie, it is fine."

"Do you hear this?" My father asked the men. "She's tough, this one, always thinking she can take care of herself."

I could never figure out why mafia men viewed women as meek and inferior but it seemed that it was in their upbringing. It was always a surprise, and even repulsive, for them to see an independent woman. Most of their wives were dependent on them, and I always wondered how they would survive on their own. It wasn't what I wanted to be. I refused to depend on anyone other than myself.

I was somewhat of an outcast around the wives. Their offensive perfume, plastered makeup and large hair, the gossip, cooking and shopping, none of it really appealed to me. I had spent my younger years feeling abnormal and out of place for not being what they were and what they felt I should be. They looked at me differently, as did the men, due to my personality. As an adult, I vowed to shine as myself, even if I was different than their vision of normal.

Chapter 6

Marco had been calling me, hour after hour, for more than a week since our argument, but with my hunger for him was the lingering anger over his deception. It had become painfully obvious that I loved him too much. I had allowed myself to be lured away from my life's priority by him and it was time to get back on track, despite how much I missed him.

I was already preparing for my third trip, this time to Athens, Greece, which Georgio was accompanying me to. The plan was the same as always only, this time, we were selling heroin rather than cocaine, and we boarded the plane without a hitch.

"We have a long flight ahead of us," he commented. "Come su una bevanda?"

"Yeah, okay," I agreed. "I could use a drink to relax me." Besides, at that point, all we had was time.

"You know, Marco would kill me with his bare hands if he knew that I was here with you."

"Yeah, well, a man who has a wife and children that he keeps a secret has no place in the business of his mistress," I replied matter-of-factly. "I'm finished with him." My tough as nails attitude prevailed but I knew it was a lie. I missed Marco.

"That's the life of a Mafiosi," Georgio commented and I

was dumbfounded. "They like their women on the side."

"Mafiosi?" I echoed, in disbelief that Marco was one of them. "Marco is involved with . . ." He assumed that I had known.

"Yeah, you know, the Cosa Nostra?"

Did I ever. I knew them better than most. They were, after all, my family. I wondered what Georgio would think if he knew who he was talking to. He schooled me on the culture as if I was some clueless school girl. I was young but I was wise.

I knew that what he spoke was the truth as my thoughts traveled back to my childhood and the first glance of my father with his mistress, so publicly affectionate at a sidewalk café. She was a thin, statuesque brunette, flawless with her fashionable beauty, the complete opposite of my stubby, pale-faced mother. My father's lover had implanted a smile on his face that I had never before seen and I envisioned the end of my family. An awkward exchange of glances occurred between my parents before she rushed me away, hoping I hadn't seen him, but it was already too late. The explosion that I had expected in our house, that evening, never took place and it was, in fact, as if it had never happened. I was beyond appalled to discover my mother's acceptance of her husband's affair, and it was that very thing that lessened my respect for her. Love is blind, they say, and in her case, those words rang true. She had made him her life and, without him, she would cease to exist, at least that's how she felt. For my mother, it was still easier to turn the other cheek than to risk losing the man she loved.

"Mafia men see other women but they never leave their wives," Georgio explained, and I recalled what Ava had said to me on the phone about Marco never leaving her. Her words suddenly made sense.

It put things in perspective for Marco and me. I would always be his mistress, never worthy of his wife. She was where his commitment lay and I could either accept it or move on without him. My mother's acceptance of it had dimmed my respect so how, then, could I condone it also?

Hours later, the plane landed in Greece as my usual anxiety

set in. Airport security, especially in other countries, was always risky with the threat of being caught with drugs. I had been lucky, so far, but it was naïve to believe that it would always be easy.

"Stay calm," Georgio uttered softly to me, apparently taking notice of my growing anxiety. It was easy for him to say. The heroin wasn't in his suitcase.

The security officers appeared only to be searching random people in line and, fortunately for me, they honed in on two unlucky young men behind us, enabling my companion and me to walk through without suspicion. I breathed a sigh of relief.

"I don't know why I keep doing this," I told Georgio. "It's too risky."

"Well then, maybe it's time that you get your own runner." It meant that I had earned the right to have someone do, for me, what I was doing for Georgio. The trips I had taken had earned his trust. It was like being promoted within a corporation and I was more than keen on the idea.

My fellow traveler spared no expense on our trip as we walked through a regal lobby of the premier Athens resort and I wondered why I hadn't been granted such luxurious accommodations on my previous trips. I stood, in awe, at the glass wall that surrounded the massive swimming pool amid the glorious mountains on the outside.

"It's our honeymoon so we would prefer not to be disturbed," I heard Georgio tell the desk clerk.

"Certainly," she replied with a naughty grin. "Enjoy your stay, Mr. and Mrs. Armisi." His sentiment was, somehow, arousing to me. Mr. and Mrs. had a nice ring to it, even if it was a lie.

The suite housed an immaculate living room fireplace and luxurious couches of gold and blue, housed in golden hued walls and velvet, blue carpets with a bathroom of white marble. It was a room fit for a king and I felt just like royalty.

"This is gorgeous," I said but, for him, the luxury was normal. It was how Georgio was used to living and he wouldn't have accepted anything else.

"We're meeting our contact in one hour and then going

straight to dinner so get dressed," he said. "Wear something nice."

I have to admit that it was my first time dressing up for a deal. In one stocking beneath my skirt was the cold steel of my .45 and it felt sexy, dangerous.

The driver turned into the circular, brick driveway of a Greek millionaire, where two suited guards met us, one of whom led us through a maze of antique and art-accented rooms until we came to an indoor pool, where the man in his fifties was swimming laps like an Olympian.

"Aren't you early?" He asked us with astonishment of our arrival.

"Actually, we're right on time," I answered.

"Who is she?" He peered at me, demanding to know from Georgio, as if I didn't belong there with him.

"It's okay, she's my partner", he casually and quickly replied. "Let's do this deal."

"She is the αστυνομία."

"Do I look like a cop?" I asked him. "Are you ready, or not, because we're running out of time?"

"Let's go to my office," the man suggested after climbing out of the water and putting on his robe and, with the bodyguard, we followed him there, where he opened his safe full of cash.

I watched him toss eighteen bundles of bills on his desk.

"Where's the other two?" I probed matter-of-factly.

"It is there," the egotistical-toned man insisted and I was fed up with his facade. I calmly pulled out my gun and aimed.

"Don't patronize me like I'm stupid," I warned him. "I'm done playing games, so you put up the other ten thousand and we'll do the deal so we can leave." I spoke like a professional of the game.

"Okay, okay," he surrendered with his hands in the air. "Here it is." Inside, I grinned with immense satisfaction, though my poker face remained.

"Thanks, and here you go," I succumbed to his request. "You have a fantastic day."

"You're crazy, ragazza," Georgio told me at dinner. "You

didn't need me at all."

Returning his grin and with a sip of wine, I joked, "I never invited you."

"You impressed me. I never expected that, given the way that you were talking after the last trip, but it was foolish. That man had a crew of armed guards at his disposal."

If he had known what our previous contacts had put me through, he would've surely understood, I thought. Georgio went on to explain that my "jobs" had earned me the right to move up in rank and employ someone to run the trips for me, and I was more than willing to accept the offer.

His words, somehow, gave me a sense of power and, inside of me, I felt it. It was a feeling that nourished my very famine. All I had ever craved in life was power, respect and I was finally achieving it. My unofficial induction into the Sicilian Mafia was, for me, like being home.

It's true, the Cosa Nostra had always been family to me and, with them, an unspoken loyalty. I could go to any one of them, at any time, for a favor, except for a piece of the business. The Sicilian Mafia just didn't allow a person, especially a woman, to walk in and pull rank. Everyone started at the bottom and there were no exceptions. Women entering the ranks was never an option so I was breaking the rules, even if I had earned my way in. As I mentioned before, in those days, Sicilian men ruled with superiority and it was their firm belief that women were incapable of handling business matters. Not only were we lacking the education but they deemed us far too emotional to handle the responsibilities. In their eyes, our place was in their shadows. That's how it had always been and it's what the female population had adopted as law, except for me, of course. I had penetrated their barrier and found my way in, thanks to Georgio, and I appreciated him for recognizing my abilities rather than gender, even if was more for his own benefit. It was amusing to hear him, egotistically, raving about his own power within the clan in a poor attempt to electrify me, and still fully unaware that I was the boss's daughter. I wasn't at all impressed, knowing full well that he was no more than a lowly associate for the true power within the empire but, even so, he was my ticket in. I could further infiltrate myself from there. I could feel the influence overflowing inside of me and it only intensified with each glass of wine. The excitement had overtaken me and I couldn't sit still any longer. I needed a release.

"Let's go dancing!" I exclaimed, almost losing track of my purpose there. "I need to do something."

I would be lying to say that he took advantage of me, since I was anything but powerless, but Georgio's seductive dark eyes, peering hungrily into mine, somehow caressed me with a mysterious touch. His lips were suddenly different, inviting. They demanded my attention, though with the essence of a gentle dove. His stare whispered delicate sentiments of passion that awakened my soul, even healing my fresh wounds inflicted by Marco.

I struggled to breathe with my fluttering stomach that suddenly yearned for him as he glared into me with intensity, deeming it, seemingly, impossible to remove our eyes from one another, the mutual look that screamed "I need you."

"Shall we go?"

"I'm ready," I replied, though I'm sure it was emitted as more of a seductive mutter. We exited with his hand gently cradling my hip. Even my walk grew sexier in his grasp. I felt irresistible to him.

Barely out of the door, Georgio pinned me against the wall with his lips passionately on mine, his powerful hands implanted firmly on my hips as he kissed me with a ravishing force. I have to admit that his aggression fed my excitement, though I wasn't usually keen on public displays of affection. Perhaps, that night, it was the wine or a strange city that relinquished my compliance but, whatever the reason, it thrilled me with ecstasy at that moment. Stricken with inhibition, something within me needed him more than anything else in the world. He was a magnet, drawing me to him with uncontrollable force, and I was ready to relish in his fervor.

Inside the limo, my lover instructed the chauffer to keep driving and then rolled up the tinted window that separated him from us. With our newfound privacy, Georgio, graciously revealing his bronzed and rippled physique, began his gradual tour of my body, a journey of passionate quivers that traveled through my entirety, time and time again. The rhythmic gyrations of his hips, tantalizing my senses, set my body ablaze with erotic explosions as I screamed out for the world to hear.

It was better than I had ever before experienced, our encounter, and I felt cleansed, rejuvenated as a new woman. Never before had I felt so replenished and satisfied.

"That was incredible, Marc . . ." I slipped before I could stop myself. "Georgio I meant," I stammered. "I'm sorry. I didn't mean that." I had just committed the ultimate lovers' sin and I felt like a heel. How could I even be thinking of Marco after his betrayal? He had blatantly deceived me, leading me to believe in the ultimate love, that which is desperate and without boundaries and of which he vowed to me. I could only dismiss my cruel comment as mere habit.

"Really, it's okay," Georgio claimed but his face outplayed his words. Maybe it shouldn't have mattered since we weren't an item anyway but, somehow, it did matter, not only to him but also to me, even given my history with Marco, my painful sentiment mattered.

"It isn't not okay because he's trash and you aren't," I told him and my words were sincere. Staring into my eyes, once again, he kissed me softly, with a sentiment of love.

"Thank you," he said as we headed back to the hotel.

That night, Georgio lay in bed with me, his arms cradling me in his warmth, and I was amazed by his comfort. His arms were suddenly where I was meant to be. I wasn't just filling an absence. I truly felt something with Georgio but I feared that he didn't. Maybe I was just simply there for the moment. One crazy night had changed me, my thoughts, feelings, even my future, and I wondered how one man, who I barely even knew, could invoke that. In his arms, I turned and felt his breath on my face as I massaged my fingers through his satin hair. His soft lips found mine in the darkness and I kissed him like I loved him, meshing my body tightly into his. His arms strengthened around me as we pulled our bodies as close together as possible while, still, I felt like I couldn't get close enough. Maybe it was my fear of losing him. We made love as an unspoken combination of adoration and need, our bodies yearning for the touch of the other, nourishing the starvation of two lost souls.

"I need you, Francesca," Georgio moaned and I wanted to say that I needed him, too, but I couldn't get out the words. He brought to me the pleasures of my womanhood that trembled through every ounce of my body in replenishment of my very soul. No other man could please me the way that Georgio did.

"You're so incredible," I complimented breathlessly.

"You are incredible," he responded. "I want this. I want you to be mine, Francesca."

I wanted to be his, too, but the love that lingered for Marco would never permit it. Intimate is all that Georgio and I could ever be and from that feeling came only silence. Cradled in his arms, I found myself grieving. Marco had made a fool of me as if what we had meant nothing, our relationship an emotionless fling to him. He had made a mockery of my love for him and his wife was his selection. Why, then, did I still pine for him, the security of his embrace, the thrill of his kiss, even the warmth of his voice? I missed the vision of my future in his eyes. In Georgio, a wealth of adoration awaited me but something wouldn't let me live without my first love.

"What are you thinking about?" My lover softly enquired with a tender gaze. "Don't tell me. I already know."

"I'm sorry," I sighed. "I do try not to think of him."

"Marco already has his life, Francesca."

"I know he does," I responded, wishing I had only known it before falling for him.

"So why not take a chance on me?" Georgio asked. "I don't expect you to love me, already, but I can be good for you and we can build something together."

He was right. He deserved a chance. Marco had already decided the fate of our relationship and, perhaps, it was time to move on. Besides, I had more in common with Georgio. He was closer to my age and we were both headed in the same direction in life, a career in the Cosa Nostra.

"I really do like you, Georgio," I told him. "Let's just take it day by day." It was truly all that I could give him at that moment.

The next morning, we boarded the plane with the dirty money that we had earned, money that told a story of lies and deceit amid the hands of thieves. It would travel from the bad to the worst and I was the one delivering it there.

My next order of business was a new recruit for our endeavors and my selection needed to be made delicately. I needed someone that I could trust, completely, a soldier who proved clever and brave, loyal and dedicated, yet still someone who didn't look the part. I needed someone with a face of innocence and, with that, my extensive search began.

My trips had earned me the wealth for new investments and, since I no longer worked for Marco, I started my own "loan company", lending money to people who couldn't get bank loans for various reasons, imperfect credit or income verification, perhaps. I always had funds available but the interest was high and the loans were short term. The true beauty of my business was being exempt from the mafia getting their cut of the proceeds, a perk of being the boss's daughter.

"This is trouble," my father warned. "You do not belong in this lifestyle. How will you enforce payment?" His concern was already taken care of with the strong-armed soldiers that I had hired, enforcers that would ensure payments through punishment. In the Cosa Nostra, a business's lack of payment called for penalties, things happening to the business, perhaps a few broken windows or a sudden fire. Mafiosi always got their payoff, through one avenue or another.

"I got it covered, Papa," I reassured him, but he made it clear that he didn't like my activities.

"I forbid this, Francesca!" He declared but I refused to give in. "I'll put some men on it." If he couldn't stop me then he would ensure the protection of me and my interests.

"Papa, please, I can handle this. Can you just make sure I don't get taxed?"

"Okay," he surrendered, "no cut for us." Pride tinted my father's eyes. "You drive a hard bargain," he added with a smirk, and it made me beam. I knew that he was only permitting my activities because I was his daughter.

With Georgio's help, I found an ambitious and innocent looking woman eager to take over my trips. Lenora Caperelli was an attractive and brazen woman in her late thirties. Her suave confidence vowed her ability to handle dangerous situations and it helped that she had done some previous work for Georgio. She looked like a librarian in all of her plainness, which was exactly what I needed. Assured to be competent and trustworthy, I made her my new subordinate.

A couple of weeks later, a familiar knock greeted my front door and I opened it to find a dismal looking Marco. I peered at him suspiciously with a pre-programmed attitude, though my heart disguised all of its old feelings rushing back in.

"Can I come in?" His tone was frail, that of an apologetic child who had betrayed another. I allowed my former lover inside, though reluctantly, given the events of our previous encounter. Even still, I yearned to hear his words. I needed him to profess his love, his dire need for me. I wanted to see him pine for my affection, labeling himself a fool for allowing my escape. Through my glass of Pinot Gris, I observed a vulnerable kitten nursing his wounds. "Francesca, I'm sorry," he began, "for everything I've put you through." His sincere eyes wasted no time confiscating my breath. "I didn't intend to fall for you like I did. Truthfully, you began as a fling, something exciting in my lifeless marriage, but I messed up because I let myself fall in love." He gulped back his tears with a sigh. "You didn't deserve what I did and I lost you because of it. I lost you to Georgio and it kills me inside because you were meant to be mine." Never before had I seen Marco so vulnerable and the sincerity of it touched me. As much as I coached myself not to fall for his charm, my racing heart was steadily gaining control.

"Marco, I . . ."

"No, Francesca, you don't have to say it," he interrupted. "I just need you to know how I feel because, truly, the best times of my life were all with you."

I know, at this point, you're probably thinking, why didn't he just leave his wife to be with me if his love was, in fact, so profound? That just didn't happen back then, for two reasons. It was considered very dishonorable, a mortal sin, for an Italian man, especially a Mafiosi, to abandon his family for any reason and, secondly, a mafia wife always knew too much that could easily be used against him if she felt betrayed. The men of the Cosa Nostra, even in the worst of marriages, didn't leave their wives, though nearly all of them were known to have a mistress or two. With Marco, all I could ever be was second best, forever walking in the shadow of his wife. It was a lifestyle that I just couldn't accept. I deserved a man who would make me his first priority, a man like Georgio, who was willing to devote himself to me completely.

"I'll always feel something for you, Marco, but the truth is that I'm nobody's mistress," I said. "For me, it's all or nothing." His head hung grievously with the finality of my words. It was the silent ultimatum that he resisted. Marco was the kind of guy who truly felt that he could have both his wife and me. For one of us to force a decision from him was nothing short of preposterous.

"You know I can't let you go, Francesca," he told me. "You are my drug."

"The choice is no longer yours," I replied casually, but my words betrayed me with pain.

"You need to know that Georgio has never been loyal to any woman." It was Marco's last attempt to keep me in his grasp. Maybe he was right.

"I guess I'm lucky, then, that I don't need either of you," I fibbed in my rugged persona.

"Don't ever forget that I love you," Marco said before walking out the door a broken man. I loved him, too, and desperately and, as hard as it was to let him walk out of my life, I was proud of my strength as he did. Besides, I had business to focus on and he was one less distraction.

Chapter 7

My new business venture proved an immediate success that even my father was proud of. I had several hundred thousand lira loaned out and was receiving thousands back each month in payments and interest. It made for a comfortable lifestyle of luxury and gratification. I was a walking ATM and, because of it, I had two full-time bodyguards near me at all times, as well as security at my house, a full staff of Mafiosi to protect me and my assets.

Lenora, meanwhile, was preparing for a trip to Austria. Her extensive coaching and prior success eased my anxiety and permitted my trust but the risk was never to be forgotten. This trip would be different than those before it. If we pulled it off, we would triple the amount of money and take fewer trips. More money, less risk. For us, it was a win-win situation.

"You know the game," I told her. "Play cool, play smart." Lenora was going for a major purchase of cocaine. Her goal was to bring back a quarter of it in the suitcase, part securely packaged and shipped to me in an anonymous name and the rest would be put in a train car. Since the railroads were commonly intercepted by the Cosa Nostra anyway, it would be extremely easy to accomplish. "I will have someone there to pick up the packages," I assured her.

"I feel good. I'm ready," my plainly-dressed associate nodded with a cleansing breath.

"Hey," I peered firmly into her eyes, "this is the grande, the big one. Don't crack." I couldn't deny my growing anxiety over the risk but there was no place for it. We were confident and experienced enough to pull it off, and all we had to do was play smart.

I drove Lenora to the airport and headed out to meet Georgio for dinner. My life was one of privilege, graciously allowing the finer aspects, and expensive dinners were certainly no exception.

This was a restaurant in a nearby resort that I had visited once before, and I remembered it well because of its exceptional cuisine and atmosphere. Georgio sat, fashionably clad in his Armani suit, with a glass of wine, awaiting me. He was so handsome, the exotic looking model type, with his muscular build, Adam's apple and firm jaw line accenting his bronzed skin. He was always well-dressed and manicured, overly attentive to his hygiene, and he smelled as good as he looked, emitting a sex appeal that, somehow, seemed to captivate me. Georgio never had a problem attracting women. He was a magnet, luring them into his mysterious dark eyes.

"Well, hello," I said as he rose up from his chair to greet me with a kiss. I felt the envy of the other women who observed us. He had the aura of a hero and the aroma of bliss that claimed my senses.

"What a beautiful sight you are, as always," my companion complimented as he pulled out my chair. He poured me a glass of wine as I glanced out at the mirrored sea through the bay window. The fireplace was aglow with the soothing crackle of its flame and the candle illuminated his features with perfection in the dimmed room that sang of romance.

"How was your trip to the airport?" He enquired.

"Uneventful, thankfully, and we can pick up the packages

in a few days." I responded. I needed a relaxed evening to rid myself of the anxiety I felt over Lenora's trip.

"I spoke to Marco today," he commented in a sudden change of subject. "He told me that he went to see you and, well, he's pretty upset with me, as you can imagine."

"I'm sorry. I never wanted to come between friends." It was true. I had fallen into my relationship with Georgio, blindly, never thinking of its effects on anyone else. What innocently began as business had quickly evolved into love.

"He will get over it and we'll remain friends," Georgio said. "Marco is already married. He can't offer you anything and it tortures him that I can. He feels like I stole you away from him."

"You couldn't have stolen something that wasn't his," I told him. "I deserve a chance to be happy and with you, I am."

Georgio raised his glass for a toast. "Here's to a promising future together, both business and personal." I concurred with a wink and a smile.

"Salute," I replied.

The day and a half that followed felt like the longest of my life. My body was enrapt with anxiety and fear over Lenora's trip. I worried about her safety and sanity, hoping that she could pull off the deal, like we had planned, and I began to feel like I should have gone with her. Part of me wanted to call her but it was imperative to keep our correspondence to emergencies and, besides, I thought, it was business not friendship. There was no room for compassion in this game.

No matter what I did to repel it, I was plagued with fear, panic threatening to take over. I tried watching television, reading, even visiting my parents but my mind was on that deal and, most times, I found myself pacing the floor of my living room, the stress gnawing on me like a leech, hungrily stealing my blood. This was the opportunity of a lifetime for Lenora and me but the risk nearly outweighed the wealth. We couldn't afford even one small mistake. The game needed to be played with a vigilant strategy.

I recruited a couple of guys that I had grown up with in my old neighborhood who would help unload some of the cocaine to some smaller dealers in town while two other trusted contacts of mine would sell directly to the larger players, Mafiosi and businessmen mostly, and, truthfully, that's where the real money would be made. Cocaine equaled big business in those days and Sicily was a large player in the game at that time. Eighty percent of the Cosa Nostra's revenue was in trafficking cocaine all around the world.

My route to pick up Lenora from the airport rendered me grateful for the relief form the sleepless nights and floor treading. It was imperative that our plan went smoothly and we were already halfway there. If we could finish the deal, we would be home free.

Her plane landed and I watched the travelers flow from it, hoping that she had made it through customs. One by one, people emptied the plane but none were Lenora. Panic set in and my face seared with trepidation while sweat beaded at my hairline. I scrambled to escape the airport as quickly as possible, hoping that security wasn't looking for me, but I had no idea what to do. I needed to find out where Lenora was but hanging around the airport was just too risky.

I had given her a temporary cell phone and prepaid minutes and, though communication between us was risky, I reluctantly dialed the number.

"Ciao?" She answered.

"Hi, did you miss the plane?"

"Si, I'm sorry," Lenora confirmed. "I tried to call but couldn't reach you. I'll be on the next one at sette."

As you can imagine, I was agitated, to say the least. How could I return for her in four hours when I had to meet my contact at the train depot for the shipment there? I had no choice but to enlist Georgio's help. While he went to pick up Lenora from the airport, I drove to the depot.

"It's here," my contact, a maintenance worker for the railroad, informed, leading me to a utility room. Just as planned, in the corner were two sealed wooden crates, carefully packaged and containing large, cocaine-packed Austrian statues.

"Great doing business with you," I told him after we loaded

the crates into the van I had rented under a bogus name. I handed him an envelope with three thousand lira for his help, which lit up his eyes.

"Oh, anytime, anytime," he graciously replied and as I opened the car door to get in, he probed further. "What's in there, anyway?"

With a grin, I thanked him again and drove back to my house. Lenora and Georgio would be stopping off at an abandoned house to make the exchange of goods before Georgio returned to my place.

"I've got it," he told me and I could finally breathe. There was only one package left and it would be picked up at the postal station the next day.

In one corner of my bedroom, a built-in bookcase discreetly opened to a small room, a closet, where a portion of the floor opened to reveal an underground safe. Only two things were ever kept there – money and things that were worth money – and the only two who knew about it were me and the contractor who I hired to install it.

We had forty kilos and ten more to get.

"Where do you want it?" Georgio asked me.

"Let's just put it in this suitcase in my closet for now," I told him. "I'll take care of it later."

A short time later, the two of us sat with our glasses of wine when the doorbell rang. We peered, nervously at each other, wondering who could be there at eleven o'clock at night. My parents would never make an unannounced visit that late and the only other possibility I could think of was the police. Surely, we were busted, I thought. We sat in fearful silence as a loud knocking began. My heart raced through a nervous rumble within me and panic kidnapped my sanity. The knocking grew louder and more rapid.

"Francesca, are you there?" The muffled voice probed.

"Marco?" I softly asked myself. I wondered what he wanted as I opened the door to a man with wrinkled clothes, ragged hair and squinted eyes. "What are you doing here?"

"What's he doing here?" He interrogated with slurred words and a betrayed eye on Georgio.

"He's your friend, Marco, and you're obviously drunk," I said to him and, against my better judgment, invited him in.

"I want to talk to you," Marco told me.

"I'll give you some time," Georgio offered, leaving the room.

"Why are you with him?" His slurred words were hardly legible.

"What do you want to talk to me about, Marco?" I had no patience for his jealousy issues. He plopped himself down on the sofa as if in emotional despair. It was the first time I had ever seen Marco in a drunken daze and I got the feeling that it was, somehow, triggered by problems with his wife.

"I miss you," he confessed to me and I was in no mood for a conversation about his emotional needs.

"What's going on with you?" I probed, peering at his depression. "I've never seen you like this." In truth, all I wanted to do was send him away so that I could get back to business.

"I can't stop thinking of you," he said. "I want you to be mine again." My patience was wearing thin and I realized that we were in a conversation that would go nowhere.

With an intolerant sigh, I said, "Listen, Marco, you have a wife who loves you and you need to go home to her."

"With his head in his hands, he responded, "I love you, Fran." His desolation tapered my attraction to him. Georgio eased his way back out to the living room.

"Marco, let me take you home and we'll talk about it."

He arose from the sofa with fury in his glazed eyes. "I'm not talking to you! You ruined my life!" My eyes widened with anxiety over his growing agitation. His drunken stupor had stolen his character and I wondered what he was capable of.

"You have a beautiful wife at home, my friend," Georgio responded with a surprisingly soothing tone. "Let me take you to her. She needs you."

"Francesca needs me and I will fight for her." I shook my

head in disgust at how ridiculous Marco sounded, and I was sure that he would agree if he were sober.

"No need to litigio, amico," Georgio maintained his calm voice. "Come, I will take you home."

"You're not taking me home because we're no longer friends!" He barked at Georgio. "You betrayed me and you know what that means." It meant punishment, death.

"Enough!" I intervened, in anger, as I rushed over to Marco. "You will not threaten anyone in this house because it's my turf!" My finger was pointed in his face like a mother scolding her son. "You go throw your weight around somewhere else, not here." My ex-lover's stern eyes demanded mine in an attempt at control.

"Do you know who I am?" He asserted with power. "You don't give orders to a Mafiosi." It was the first time that I had ever heard him admit his involvement and his words were a spear penetrating me.

"Oh yeah?" I replied smugly. "I do if I'm the capo's daughter."

Both men stood, stunned by my declaration that had brought the battle of egos between them to a halt. A bewildered silence infiltrated the room as Georgio and Marco absorbed my announcement, and I almost giggled at the dumbfounded faces that both wore. I had effortlessly gained control, merely by my status.

"You're Lorenzo's daughter?" Georgio echoed, still in disbelief.

"I am, so Marco, it's time for you to leave," I said and he obeyed in astonished silence.

"Why didn't you tell me?" Georgio asked. I dropped softly to the couch with a sigh.

"I'm sorry. It's just not something you tell people, for obvious reasons," I responded.

"Don't you think I need to know if I'm dating the boss's daughter?" He might have had a point.

"I just didn't want to be judged on that."

After a short silence and a snicker, he replied, "Well, I

guess it's not Marco that I need to worry about then," he ribbed but he was right.

The next morning, I got dressed to pick up the final package at the Post Office but my nerves were getting the best of me. The retrieval was risky and if I was caught, there would be no way out of it. My sweating palms accompanied a racing heart. I needed to calm myself down before I went. On my balcony overlooking the gentle ocean in the warmth of the morning sun, I sat in meditation, my eyes closed and my breathing calm and steady, in through my nose and slowly out through my mouth. Forty-five minutes had passed before I finally felt relaxed enough to go.

The Post Office was relatively quiet, with only two other people inside and I wished it was busier to help divert any attention from me, but I was ready to take my chances.

"Ciao, parcel for Rosa Mancini, please," I told the clerk as calmly as possible. My racing heart spelled anxiety while he disappeared into the back to locate it. The man returned with the box and what I deemed as suspicion on his face, and I struggled to discern if it was real or merely my fear of the worst.

"Avete identificazione?" He queried and I struggled to stay calm as I pretended to search for my identification card in my wallet.

"I'm so sorry. I must have forgotten it," I told him but he didn't appear convinced. "I always do things like this."

"I have to see it before I can release the package," he informed me and, with no other choice, I turned on the sensuality that may have, very well, been my God-given talent.

"Couldn't we let it slide, just this once?" I asked with an innocent pout. "It's such a long way back to my hotel room to get it," I fibbed, and my ploy appeared to be working. The clerk's roving eyes spoke of the possibility as he scanned my assets.

"What's in the box anyway?" He asked and I struggled to invent something that would prohibit further questioning.

"Well, actually, I'm a little embarrassed to admit that it's a package of, how should I say, feminine necessities, from home."

The perversion on his face turned suddenly to an awkwardness that so many men face with that subject, and he handed over the package. I was home free.

With the help of Georgio and Lenora, I had pulled off a colossal deal that would yield a horde of money. For me, this was a business venture. I was the manager and, under me, a few salesman making my highly demanded product more readily available. Now that the hard part was behind me, what remained seemed a breeze. My salespeople were set up with their own contacts and all I had to do was supervise.

Chapter 8

"I've been thinking that it's time to take our relationship to the next level," Georgio whispered as I lay, wrapped in his arms. Raging thoughts of panic infiltrated my mind, almost immediately. I liked our relationship just the way it was. What fueled his sudden need to escalate it?

"What's the next level?" I reluctantly responded, unsure if I wanted the answer.

"Well, I think we should try living together."

It seemed like such an enormous step, and I couldn't justify changing something that was already good. How could I live with someone else when I could barely live with myself at times? Even the thought of it smothered me. My home was my own space, my private sanctuary, where no one else was permitted.

"Why do we have to live together?" I queried. "We can see each other as much as we want already." A moment of hysteria threatened me. I felt like Georgio was trying to turn me into my mother, an obedient housewife living in a man's shadow. I relished my independence and wasn't willing to compromise it for Georgio or anyone else. As selfish as it sounds, I refused to let him invade my space.

"Why keep alternating nights at each other's houses when we can both just be in one place together?" He responded and it made perfect sense but, for me, it was still a commitment that I wasn't ready for. I sat up, staring into my lover's enticing eyes with my hand caressing his cheek.

"You're such an amazing person, tesoro, but please understand that I'm just not ready yet." I was sure that my words stung and, though I didn't want to hurt him, I knew that I had.

In silence, he got out of my bed and got dressed. Already, I had lost him.

"What are you doing?" I asked him but I already knew.

"I love you, Francesca," he said, "but I won't give my soul to someone who doesn't give hers to me, so you call me when you figure out what you want." With that, Georgio walked out the door and out of my life.

I was left with a heavy heart over losing a man that I cared so deeply for and I knew that he loved me, but I was forced to take my feelings at face value. Part of me fought to reconsider the decision that I had made and try living with Georgio. Perhaps it would be the best decision that I could ever make. Still, the larger part of me wouldn't permit it.

I couldn't focus on love. My life was business. It was my priority and the source of my success. Already, I had a team of several employees, all with different duties to fulfill. My salesmen sold the drugs while three others collected loan payments. I also employed a couple of enforcers to ensure payment from the goons who tried to stiff me was made. Little by little, I had earned my place, and my respect, in the Cosa Nostra and, as long as we weren't stepping on the toes of my father's army, we were good as gold.

All that my parents knew was that I was a loan shark and, though it wasn't their ideal career choice for me, I had inherited my father's stubborn "I'll do what I want" mentality. Reluctantly, my parents had accepted my decision.

It didn't take long for Lenora's trip to pay off. Thousands

of lira were coming in each week and I used my portion to buy a couple of buildings in town, which I planned to lease out to businesses. It was no secret that nearly everything was owned by the mafia so it became that I began working with my father on a few of the deals and, just the same, my properties were protected by him. It wasn't my father's preference for me to be involved, in any form, with mafia activities and, in fact, I wasn't permitted to hold a position within the same "family" as a relative of an existing officer, nor as a woman, but I had always been a rule breaker and I suppose that at least, this way, he could, somehow, safeguard me. Had it not been for me being the boss's daughter, I would have faced serious consequences for operating on my own and, still, I'm lucky I didn't.

It went without saying that my mother remained as clueless as possible about our activities. Her reputation as a worrier assured us that the less she knew, the better and, though she was aware of my work, my business with my father and the Cosa Nostra was discreetly kept from her.

Business with my father was kept solely to the properties that I owned. He knew nothing about the drugs and I didn't want him to, but I often wondered if he knew more than he let on. Surely, he was smart enough to know that my properties, alone, weren't enough to bring in the cash that I had. Even so, what could he really say about it, given his own activities?

Being without Georgio had ushered in the dire need for companionship. My "business" was a success but I needed some fun and I craved the masculine touch of a man. The temptation to call Georgio prevailed but I needed someone with no strings attached. Georgio was adamant about commitment but, after the heartbreak that I had been through with Marco, it wasn't what I was looking for. Truth be told, a one-night stand was all that I was willing to make time for and, though I had never been that type of girl, I preferred a stranger who would go home afterward over another dramatic circumstance.

Clad in my sexiest black mini dress and favorite perfume, I drove to a nightclub that I had recently bought. The music lent an energetic bliss amid the neon lasers beaming across the crowded dance floor and it bred life into the grinning patrons. I squeezed through the mass, making my way to the circular oak bar, the magnificent centerpiece where so many gathered.

"Ah, Miss Francesca, to what do I owe the pleasure?" The handsome, blond bartender welcomed with a kiss on my hand.

"It would be my pleasure to take you home with me," I thought, jokingly, but I wouldn't dare utter it. Still, I was there on a mission, with solely one goal in mind.

"Just needed to get out for a little fun," I replied to my employee's question. "What do you have good to drink behind this bar?"

"Depends on how much fun you want to have."

"Well, how about Sex on the Beach?" I requested with a lighthearted wink, to his amusement.

"Anytime," he grinned and made me the drink. I found myself with a fluttering stomach as I dreamed of the possibilities with such an appealing man but I was quickly brought back to the reality of me as his boss. I had to move on.

After two shots of Tequila and with a drink in my hand, I scoured the establishment, a cougar after her prey, and, to my surprise, it took no effort at all. The men were plentiful, each vying for my attention and overly eager to share his night with me, and there were so many that the choice became overwhelming. Something that should have come so easily for me quickly grew unsatisfying and I knew that it was the absence of the challenge. How can a cougar stalk her prey when it's placed at her feet? My sudden disinterest sent me home alone.

As circumstance would have it, I arrived home to hear my phone ringing.

"Hello?" I answered to hear Marco's voice.

"Feel like company?" He asked me as if he'd forgotten our last conversation and, still somewhat incensed at his former actions, my instincts commanded my refusal. Still, my need for a man's touch, his touch, won the battle and I found myself inviting him over.

I knew it was wrong and I had already changed my mind by the time he showed up. I was already making the mistake.

"I've missed you," he told me. The words that I once craved now sounded bizarre and it was a lesser part of me that missed him. What once felt so familiar had become alien to me. "This is how it's meant to be, Fran," Marco said with my hands in his, "you and me." This time, it was different for me. The yearning that I once felt was gone. I didn't look at him the same way. He was almost a stranger again and I was relieved. His lips near mine forced me to pull away.

"I'm sorry," I uttered with my eyes shamefully aimed at the floor.

"What's wrong?" He probed but a sigh was all that I could muster. I felt the guilt rush in. Why had I allowed him in my house again knowing that he would arrive with expectations that I couldn't fulfill?

"I just can't and I'm sorry," I told him. "I really thought I could." I witnessed the disappointment transform Marco's face.

"Your feelings for me are gone?"

"Tonight they are," I told him.

Time was beginning to lend memories of Georgio and, with it, the painful absence of him. My unreasonable fear of commitment was hardly worth the loss that I was feeling, and I realized that forcing him out of my life was the worst mistake I had ever made. What was I so afraid of that would allow him to walk out of my life rather than share a home together?

I wanted to run to my lover, proudly professing my love like Juliet with her Romeo. This time, I was really ready for the commitment. In my little silk sundress and his favorite perfume, I drove across town to his house to surprise him. Finally, I was ready to surrender myself, completely, to the man I loved.

My heart raced in my path to his door and as I knocked, I prepared myself for his arms.

"Francesca," he uttered as if I had caught him off guard. He slid out onto the front porch rather than inviting me inside. "Wow, hi," he said. "I, um, I wasn't expecting to see you."

"I know," I told him, taking his hands in mine and gazing nervously into his eyes. "I've finally realized what I lost. I can't let the man I love walk out of my life and I'm not afraid anymore." Georgio looked stunned as he stared, speechless, into my eyes and it told me that something was wrong.

"Really?" He responded with a grin, "I'm so . . ."

"Innamorato, Georgio," a seductive female voice intervened from inside and I was immediately breathless, suffocating with embarrassment and anger.

"I'm sorry," I hardly got out before awkwardly escaping the moment.

"Wait!" He called out but I didn't acknowledge his plea.

It felt like I couldn't drive away quickly enough and, when I finally found my way back home, the tears of heartbreak ensued. I was furious at myself for assuming that Georgio would halt his social life to pine for me. How could I have expected him not to move on? He had, apparently, done just that. Time was no friend of mine. Just when I had finally realized that I loved someone, he had found another.

"Stop crying, you fool," I scolded myself. "It's just a man, not my life."

It was only a short time later that the knock came on my door. I opened it to find Georgio.

"Francesca, I'm so sorry," he said. "It's not at all what you think." Relief began its consolation as I allowed him in. "Yes, it was a date and only my first since you. We went to dinner and back to my place for a glass of wine and a little conversation. Nothing else happened, nor was it going to." I appreciated his explanation. "Please understand, Francesca, I thought it was over between you and me."

"I do understand and I'm sorry," I told him. "I shouldn't have expected you to wait for me, and I guess I just assumed that it was too late to love you." I took his hands in mine, locked in his brown eyes. "I love you, Georgio, and I want to make the commitment with you. I can't be without you any longer." A gracious smile warmed his face.

"I can't tell you how that makes me feel because, for me, you're the only woman in the world." His satin lips graced mine softly and passionately. Georgio was mine again and it felt right. I was complete.

Chapter 9

It was business, as usual, until I heard about one of my runners being badly beaten.

"A couple of the capo's guys did it," he confessed and, by that, he meant my father. "They got the money, too." I was fuming to the point where I felt my head would explode. My small clan didn't compare, by far, to my father's but I protected them, just the same, and I refused to allow his men to push mine around, especially after he'd already vowed our protection.

"I'll take care of this," I assured my runner. Straightaway, I called my father, insisting on seeing him.

"I'm in the middle of . . ."

"I don't care what you're in the middle of," I interrupted. "I need to see you now!" The silence that followed told me that he realized my seriousness.

"Okay," he finally agreed. We met at an empty car wash that he owned.

"Okay, innamorata, what's so important?" He probed, and his attitude was one of indifference.

"Your men attacked Armani," I snapped.

"Yeah, so what?"

"Dad, he was working for me!" It was a revelation he didn't know. I had just confessed my involvement in the drug trade.

"What? Working for you?" He was stunned, just as I imagined he would be when he found out. "What did I tell you? I told you not to get involved in that." I could see his disappointment in me but I didn't care at that moment. "Listen, if this is a business conversation, then you have to understand that your runner was in my territory, doing business without my permission," he responded firmly. "My guy didn't know him. He was just doing his job." My father had a valid point that I found difficult to argue, but I was far more taken aback by his focus being on territory rather than his daughter's mafia business. "I'm not going to start making exceptions just because you're my daughter. If you want to play the game, then you play by my rules."

"They took the money, too." I understood the rules about stepping on a Mafiosi's toes. There were always consequences for it. "He went too far, trying to make a point."

"He didn't take anything," he casually brushed off my allegations. "Your runner is trying to cop the money for himself." It was the first time that my father spoke to me as a business associate, rather than his daughter and, even as strict a parent as he was, the mafia boss was far more intimidating.

"You know he took it," I replied. "They don't do anything that you don't order." His eyes were as fire, infuriated by my revolt. I feared that the capo's role would take precedence over my father's. His actions made it clear that I was playing a deadly game. He wouldn't tolerate disrespect from anyone, including me, and there I stood, my luck running short as my heart pounded in fear. Never before had I faced my father with such disrepute.

He glared at me with uncertain eyes and I prepared myself for a lashing. I was no longer his precious daughter but a rebellious foe of his army. No one had ever disrespected the mafia boss the way that I had just done and it left him unsure how to handle it.

"I should have you working for me," he uttered, almost

with a proud smirk on his face. "You're stubborn as a mule but you've got guts of steel and the heart of a lion. What can I say, you get it honestly." He gleamed at me with a newfound sense of reverence that made me proud of myself. "No one has ever stood up to me, and your valor has earned my respect."

As relieved as I was at that moment, I had to continue my quest. "I'm here for the respect and the money back." My eyes were cold and my face stern as I spoke matter-of-factly. I couldn't mistake his ease for friendliness, and I refused to permit it to distract me from my goal.

"You're taking this too far now," he replied with a stronger tone and as fearful as I was, I maintained my glare on him. He took a deep breath and said, "Alright. You drive a hard bargain but the fact remains that your runner deserved the consequences. He was doing business there without my permission so he got what he got. I'll give back half the money."

"He's learned his lesson and I want all of the money," I insisted, unsure where my newfound power was coming from.

"No, half of the money back and you keep him out of here," my father responded. "That's the consequences for breaking the rules. You're lucky I'm in a good mood."

"Fine, done." I hadn't achieved, fully, what I had set out to do but I was proud of what I had accomplished – the respect of the mob boss – my father.

"You know, you're pretty scary sometimes," he joked as we were leaving. "You're coming for dinner on Sunday? Your mother is making her famous lasagna." Just like that, he was my dad again. With him, that's how it was. Business was business and family was family, but never were the two intermingled, even with me.

"I'll be there," I replied with a grin and a wink as I got into my car. It appeared that he and I had established a new understanding, one that spoke of honor. I had always, as his only child, been under his thumb, thoroughly controlled by his words, but it was no longer the case. I had just gained my own independence and freed myself of his grip. We had become two families of the Cosa Nostra and, though he remained the king of the land, I had earned an acre that was mine.

I operated in a very small part of town, as opposed to the large portion that my father ran, but I maintained every angle of opportunity. My runners did the drug deals while my money men collected the rent payments from the businesses, including those I didn't own. In our world, you paid to do business in mafia territory and the favor was returned with protection of your business and your family, like a service was being offered for the money. There's no doubt that I did my dirt but, just the same, it was accomplished with a bit more compassion than on my father's side. It was a strategy of success that made my part of town the preference of its people. I had turned the slums into the suburbs, where it was safe, tidy and friendly. Everyone abided by the same rules, my rules, and our community grew very tight-knit.

Sundays were always left open for family dinners at my parents' house and almost always included Mafiosi. The mobsters were family, too, after all, and an open invite was always there for the closest to my father. Nothing had changed since I was a kid. It was always the same people, the same ritual and the same conversations and just as with the years of my adolescence, I still didn't belong with the obnoxious talkers who gossiped freely amongst themselves as they cleaned up the kitchen. I always preferred the "business" of the men, who sat smoking cigars in the den but, even though I was one of them, it was clear that I was to stay with my own gender, especially since my mother still had no knowledge of my dealings.

One Sunday, I decided to take Georgio to dinner and introduce him to my parents. He knew my associations and who my father was and, though he had always been involved in the mob, he was too low on the totem pole to have ever spoken directly with my father or any of his direct associates. My father had ultimately approved each and every player in his clans, composed of several families, but many he didn't know at all and Georgio was one of them.

"Don't be nervous," I said to my trembling lover on the

way to meet my parents.

"They don't even know about me," he uttered, "not to mention that your father is Lorenzo Mazonelli, a man who could have me whacked in the blink of an eye."

"I could have you whacked just the same, so don't break my heart and you won't have to worry about it," I joked. "Listen, my father and I have an understanding so you have nothing to worry about."

We pulled into the circular, cobblestone driveway that wound past a majestic fountain and perfectly manicured gardens. Georgio's eyes indulged the enormous concrete mansion as he struggled to shake off his anxiety. I made sure to arrive a little early so that my boyfriend could be introduced without a scene.

"I can't believe I'm about to meet Capo," Georgio uttered. "How many people can say that?"

Inside the double oak doors, we made our way across the grey and pink-hued marble floors to the kitchen, where my mother, in her thin, faded apron, slaved over her famous Pasta Primavera and homemade bread that emitted a splendid aroma.

"Mama, ciao," I greeted her with a kiss on the cheek. She peered at my companion with uncertainty, surely wondering who he was. "This is Georgio, my boyfriend." Her bewildered eyes analyzed him.

"È molto nice to meet you, Mrs. Mazonelli," Georgio said with a soft kiss of her hand and a smile.

"Very nice to meet you, too." He had won her smile.

"Is Papa home?" I asked her and she directed me upstairs. "Wait here," I directed Georgio before going up to see my father.

"I brought a friend to dinner today and I want you to meet him," I said as he put on his cologne.

"A friend?" His tone was of suspicion.

"Ragazzo," I replied and, with that, he followed me promptly down the stairs. "This is Georgio."

"Good evening, sir, it's nice to meet you," Georgio uttered in a shaky tone with his hand extended. Rather than a handshake, he received a careful examination from my father. According to the commandments of the Cosa Nostra, a Mafiosi could not introduce himself to another but rather they had to be introduced solely through a third party which, in this case, was me.

"Have we met before?" He glared at my lover, almost as if he, somehow, knew him.

"I don't believe we have, sir."

"Perche haven't we met before?" He turned to ask me, obviously dismayed at my waiting so long to bring him around and before I could answer, he draped his arm around the apprehensive Georgio and directed him into the den.

"We'll be back poco," my father told me.

They still hadn't returned from the den when Vinny and Clara, Micky and Vera and the other guests began arriving, each of them greeting my mother and I with a kiss on the cheek, a greeting of respect in our Sicilian culture.

"So, Frannie, I hear you're doing a little business over on the south side of town," Bobby mentioned discreetly.

"As a matter of fact, I am."

"You've done a fantastic job over there. I'm impressed."

"Yeah, well, thanks, and you do me a favor and leave my guys alone."

"What are we, a bunch of goons?" He ribbed.

"That's exactly what you are," I replied with a snicker, and that's when my father and Georgio finally returned, both sporting smiles, to my relief.

"Hey, how ya doin', boss?" Vinny greeted my father while eyeing my date. "Who is this?"

"Ah, everybody, meet Georgio," my father announced with his arm around him. "This is Francesca's, uh, friend." Just like that, my boyfriend was part of our family and they all spoke to him as if they'd known him forever. He appeared comfortable in their midst and I watched my father stay especially close to him. Georgio seemed content under my father's wing.

Dinner was filled with the usual boisterous conversation and laughter, over pasta and wine, and I observed the way that my companion had managed to effortlessly penetrate himself into the impassable barrier of my father and his advisors. The usual ensued with the men excusing themselves to the den while the women remained in the kitchen but, that day, the gossip was me and everyone wanted to know about Georgio.

"Where did you meet him?" One asked.

"What family is he from?" Another probed. The bloodline you were derived from mattered tremendously in Sicily, at least in our part of it. The women pelted me with questions about my lover and some even revealed their envy of me. They couldn't resist hearing every detail that they could muster out of me.

"Is he good in bed?" Nina, the voluptuous and assertive wife of Mario, probed. She was a fiery-haired, overly bronzed woman in her fifties who went to extremes in an attempt to stay young, with her breast implants and botox treatments. Always outspoken, she was a no holds barred kind of person who never hesitated to ask or say what no one else dared to.

"Incredible," was my response and I swore that my mother would need to be picked up from the floor from shock since I never spoke that way in front of her. I could already see Nina fantasizing about Georgio in her mind but I couldn't really blame her since her husband had a different mistress for every day of the week and, besides, Georgio was extremely attractive.

An hour later, when the men reappeared from their cigars and Brandy, Nina instantly carved her path to Georgio, making flirtatious conversation and innuendoes with him, nearly in front of my eyes.

"Ready to go?" I interrupted with a hungry kiss on his lips before glaring at her.

"It was such a pleasure to meet you, Georgio, and I hope to see you again very soon," she commented in a seductive tone.

"Ciao, Nina," I told her, signaling her exit.

On the way home, I was dying to hear about the conversation between Georgio and my father. I had to know what he had said to earn my dad's trust so easily.

"What happened in there?" I probed.

"Well, in short, I told him I love you, and he basically

threatened to dismember me if I made even one wrong move, so we apparently see eye to eye now," he answered with a snicker.

"What? No."

"Yes, but it also came out that he and my father were closely associated some years back."

"Really?" I replied, somewhat stunned. "Where is your father now?"

"Gone. He died saving your father's life." There was immense pride on his face and shock on mine. The wheels of my car screeched to a sudden halt.

"What? Are you kidding me?" It was well-known in our household, the story of my father's life being spared by his archenemy.

Back then, they were both soldiers of the mafia, still low on the ladder and both vying for their climb to the top. It was a brutal challenge to earn one's way up in those days and both had their eyes glued to the prize. Each had committed heinous acts in the quest for promotion and it had come down to only one being granted the opportunity. Their final assignment was to rob a local liquor store and whack the owner. The one who succeeded first took a step up the ladder in the Cosa Nostra. When the owner unexpectedly pulled a gun of his own, it was Georgio's father who leaped in to take the bullet, sparing the life of my father and, as he lay dying, his words were that his deed was his respect. It was the legacy of his father that he had saved the life of mine.

I sat, my car stopped in the middle of the road, stunned at his revelation. A thousand times over I had heard that story but not once could I have imagined my father's hero being Georgio's father. It was the reason behind my father's automatic respect for my companion. My father, the mob boss, felt indebted to Georgio and would literally lay his own life down for him.

"He also offered me an opportunity to work for him," he told me and I was suddenly put out. Though I understood my father's offering to Georgio, I felt it blatantly disrespectful to me. Georgio was my partner, in business and otherwise, and my father had just slid under my radar to pilfer him. "I declined, of course," he assured me and I was grateful.

A couple weeks later, Lenora called. I hadn't spoken to her since her trip several months prior.

"I need to do another trip," she told me and I have to admit that I was taken aback. Her last one had yielded all of us a lot of money and I couldn't understand how it was already gone.

"We're not doing another one for a while," I told her. It was far too risky after the last one and I wasn't willing to push my luck or anyone else's.

"I need the money." Her voice was desperation, hopelessness and even with my compassion for her, I realized that I couldn't help everybody all the time. Still, I asked her to meet me at a local restaurant that I owned.

I had been sipping my glass of wine for twenty minutes when Lenora finally arrived, black eyeliner precluding her pale and clammy face, smudged mascara and clothes that looked thin and faded. I had never seen her so tattered.

"Thanks for meeting me," she said. "I can't stay long." She was fidgety and paranoid, frequently glancing around her evasively.

"What's going on with you?" I probed, and she peered at me in bewilderment as if she were in her normal state.

"Niente."

I leaned toward her and softened my voice. "What are you doing, Lenora?" I said. "You look like hell, and why do you need money already? You had plenty, remember?" She lowered her head into her hands and I could see the stress about her. It was obvious that the drugs had taken control of her.

"I owe some money to a guy," she finally admitted. "He's trying to kill me."

"How much?" I wanted to help her but I knew better.

"Tre," was her response and it meant three thousand lira. Nearly all of the money she had made from her trip had gone straight into her arm. She explained that she had even begun prostituting, both for the drugs and to pay back her dealers for the drugs they had already fronted her. Little by little, she was

78 | P a g e

destroying herself and part of me felt responsible.

That was always my problem as a Mafiosi. My compassion would surely get the best of me. Mobsters were ruthless and cunning. They had to be in that game but, somehow, I had that nurturing instinct that poisoned me.

"We can't do another trip right now, Lenora," I told her. Aside from the risk of being caught was the chance of her consuming all of the product. I could no longer trust her to do the right thing. "What I will do is lend you the money to pay back this guy but you're not going to evade me. This money is solely on loan and you will make payments every week on it. You miss a week, this goon will be the least of your worries, understand?"

"Grazie," she replied with a sense of relief, thanking me, but she understood the consequences and they were far worse than those of her pimp.

"Don't do this to yourself, Lenora," I told her before we parted. "That stuff you're putting into your body is ruining you." She knew I was right but the choice was hers.

The following week, when my collectors showed up, Lenora was nowhere to be found and it came as no surprise. The police found her murdered a few days later, her violently beaten and stabbed corpse in a narrow alley behind a villa known for drugs. I remember thinking what a waste it was, what the drugs had done to her, what they had allowed people to do to her. I wondered what the real purpose for her life had been. Her murder became a personal vendetta for me, not because they owed me the money, that debt was hers, but because they owed respect, respect for women, for people, and for the part of town that was run by me. My business relationship with several officers in the police department had long been established and my generous monetary contributions granted me favors by certain members. Corruption was all part of the game and no one was exempt. I had learned, long before, that anyone could be bought; everyone was for sale and fear of the Cosa Nostra was prevalent, even within the law.

"A few of my boys are going over there for some business," I informed my police contacts and they courteously looked the other way. Besides, I was ridding our end of town of its riff raff, which only made their job easier.

I sent a few of my enforcers to the villa for a lesson in respect. The four gargantuan men entered without invitation and assumed control. Who they were didn't need to be spoken because it was already clear.

"Who do you think you are?" My enforcers strong-armed all five of them by the throat. "You don't overstep your boundaries. You should know better," they said. "Don't you know what can happen to you?" The goons, in fear for their lives, began immediate apologies, vowing respect and obedience from that moment on.

"I'm not convinced," one of my guys replied. "You need to learn a little respect for who runs this part of town, you piece of garbage, and guess what? She didn't appreciate you killing that girl."

"We didn't do it," one blurted out, only infuriating my men even further.

"I should rip out your eyeballs with your own fingers for lying to me," my enforcer threatened. "The next time I have to come over here, things are going to get real messy, dirt bag, but it's your lucky day. We're going to let you live."

Before my men retreated, the five were each forced to suffer the loss of a finger to remind them of the message, and they were forced to pay a ten thousand dollar fine for the trouble they had caused.

"Next time, you won't live to tell about it," my enforcer warned.

Chapter 10

The aroma of perking coffee piqued my senses as I struggled to awaken from my groggy daze. It was eight in the morning and I turned on the news with a yawn.

"Today's top story is the arrest of infamous mobster Marco Rochelli," the attractive, dark-haired television anchor reported in her native Italian language.

"Oh my God!" I yelped, stunned at what I had just heard.

The anchor reported that Marco's house had been raided, where several kilos of heroin and a sizable stash of money had been found, along with a horde of guns. I realized the distress that it would bring to my father and to my family since arrests always sparked fears of other names being mentioned and, though the primary rule of the Cosa Nostra was to never rat out your brothers, some did in hopes of a lighter sentence. With Marco's arrest, we were all left wondering if he would take the fall or pin it on someone else. My father didn't know him, personally, but I knew that his arrest was affecting him just the same. Surely, he was questioning who tipped off the police. After all, Dad knew that Marco worked for one of his men. I went to see my parents later that morning in an attempt to feel out my father on the subject.

"He's out handling business, I guess," my mother informed me when I asked his whereabouts, and I suppose I should have expected him to be out, making preparations for the potential crackdown. I envisioned him paying some of his police contacts for information on the investigation. "He left here in a hurry this morning, didn't even eat his breakfast."

Part of me felt sorry for my mother, the blatantly methodical way that her husband excluded her from the most important part of his life. She was doomed to accept being last in his life, most of her time spent catering to her family. That was the life of a mafia wife. They were there to care for the home and family while their husbands made the money, selling their souls to the devil for the mighty dollar and gallivanting their nights away with young mistresses.

"Did Papa say when he'd be back?"

"No, but I'm sure he'll be a while. He said he had a lot to do today."

Of course he would, I thought, because strategically covering his tracks was a tedious game. I pictured him frantically consulting with Gino, Carmine, Louie and his other elite, hastily rushing to shroud their secrets. I was certain that he was preparing for the worst and I did the same. There was a lot of dirt to be covered, so to speak, and none of us could afford to leave any loose ends. I knew Marco well, and I doubted him dredging up my name, but he still held a bit of a grudge that called for me to take every precaution. All that any of us could do was wait to see what came out of his arrest.

The next day, my father called to inform me that he was on his way over to my house. He arrived with a disquieted face. His tasseled hair and weary eyes confessed his sleeplessness but, still, he played it cool.

"There's a little situation," he calmly informed me.

"I saw it on the news," I responded.

"We need to take care of some things."

As much as I didn't want my father to know about my past

with Marco, I knew that I had to tell him, given the situation. Perhaps having some insight about him would ease his mind.

"Sit down, Papa. I need to tell you something," I said. "I would have never admitted this before but, um, this guy, Marco, I know him. Lo conosco molto bene."

"What do you mean, you know him well? How well?" Concern kidnapped my father's eyes.

I took a deep breath and confessed. "I had a relationship with him. It was back when I was working at the restaurant and had just moved out. I'm only telling you this because I think he's harmless. I don't think he'll talk at all."

"I can't believe this!" My father reveled in his disappointment. "What does he know?" I watched beads of sweat gather on his forehead as his face grew red.

"Nothing other than the work he was doing for Giovanni," I told him, easing his fears. He was low in the food chain, no one to worry about." He breathed deeply as he paced in thought, calming himself as he did.

"Are you sure about this, Frannie? We need to be sure."

"Sono sicuro, Papa, positive. He's safe."

"Okay," he finally spoke, "but we still need to handle business as if he isn't. In the meantime, I'll send a little message his way." His comment meant that Marco would be threatened with his life if he ratted out his "family".

"Of course." My tone was of a soft certainty, assuring him of my confidence. I had falsified business records to account for every dollar I had made. The guns, drugs and money were removed from my house and buried miles away, by the river, and my warehouses were emptied. All of the bases had been covered and even if I was suspected, nothing could be proven.

I was reminded of a six-year span of my childhood that my father spent in prison. As a high-ranking consigliere at that time, his stint was practically a vacation with the special treatment that he received, a spacious, private cell, specially prepared meals and far more freedom and respect than any other prisoner was granted. His status even allowed him to spend the weekends at home with us. For a man like him, incarceration was a breeze. My father still conducted business, overseeing and managing daily operations from prison, even ordering hits for the boss, and very few decisions were made without his approval since he was one of only few permitted to converse directly with the Capo. His power, even within those concrete walls, was unmatched. He had the guards eating out of his hands and the prison procedures, for him, weren't the same as they were for everyone else. My father was royalty, even in prison.

If Marco squealed, my father would be back there again, but his protection was the knowledge that a pantiti faced certain death. Ratting meant that he would disappear. Besides, Marco loved the game too much to leave it. The Cosa Nostra was his life. It was all that he really cared about and his silence would earn him more power within the family.

In the next few weeks, as the attention waned, business resumed but, always, it was handled with the utmost caution. We had eyes in the back of our heads, vigilant about every move we made, but our activities continued and the money kept flowing. The police had always known about us but our power far superseded theirs and, without evidence, there were no criminals. As long as Marco kept his mouth shut, we were all safe.

Marco had infiltrated the Mazonelli crime family through Giovanni Carrazio, a runner who my father didn't know since only a select group was permitted to communicate directly with the Capo. Anyone who was brought into the family was sworn to the creed of respect and secrecy and had to be approved by a high-ranking member, these being my father's advisors. By the Commissione's policy, since Marco had been careless with mafia business, Giovanni needed to be punished so a couple of guys were sent to his apartment to rough him up.

"If Marco talks, you'll be in pieces in the river," they threatened the barely conscious warrior.

You see, the Cosa Nostra held a very stringent honor code. There were commandments, ten of them, that were always strictly adhered to, no matter what. None could ever be broken or ignored for any reason. Every single man initiated into the family knew that the rule above all others was to obey and enforce the commandments. It was the law of the Commissione that regulated the clans. The Commissione had been integrated to set standards, enforce rules and settle disputes between families. It was the government, so to speak, that all Mafiosi abided by.

Between my father and me, several provinces, the town and those nearby, were owned and run by the Mazonelli crime family. We were involved in every aspect of mafia-associated business, from drugs and gambling to extortion and murder. There wasn't a move being made that we weren't aware of or a deal that we didn't get a cut of. Our hands were in everything and our payroll included everyone from judges and police to politicians. We controlled every contract, business and deal that was happening. Everyone, it seemed, wanted a piece of the pie and we were greasing the hands of whomever we needed to in order to get what we wanted. We had more money than we even knew what to do with.

It was never necessary for a Mafiosi to boast about his status or even introduce himself to the outside world. Ours was an unspoken title and, no matter where we were or who we were with, people recognized us as power and their respect was automatic. Our presence meant control but it also offered a certain amount of protection for those who played by our rules. Perhaps not everyone thought our involvement was fair and not everyone liked us, but the bottom line was that even our enemies respected us and we lived as celebrities.

At that time, the Cosa Nostra consisted of a number of families throughout Sicily, each commanded separately by a different boss and each sworn to the omerta, the code of silence. Even among rivals, the rules were still the same and the Commissione assured that the commandments were strictly obeyed. As Mafiosi, our business consisted of many roles and activities, but there were several that were prohibited and held as a clear sign of ignorance and impertinence, things like theft, mugging or rape. They weren't acceptable in any family and if anyone was caught doing it, the punishment was severe.

There were a hundred ways to make money as a Mafiosi but, for me, the best source of income remained the pizzo, protection money. It was a big business for the mafia and, though some certainly felt it unfair, we viewed it as a service being offered, kind of like paying the government its due taxes. If you wanted to live or do business in mafia-run jurisdiction, which was everywhere, you had to pay the appropriate fees or taxes, so to speak. As long as the money was paid every month, you were left alone. It was that simple. If the money wasn't paid, faithfully, your home or business suffered the consequences through the damage it suffered each day that payment wasn't received. I had never been forced to do much more than some broken windows or busted pipes but I had seen some completely torched when too much time elapsed.

Fortunately, I had been right about Marco. He was serving his time in prison, silently, without throwing out names or information, and his loyalty to the family would serve him well after his stint. His silence was earning him a higher rank within the family as a token of appreciation and respect. As long as he kept his mouth shut, he was good as gold.

Georgio, on the other hand, had begun a power struggle of his own. Changes in his personality had surfaced and were growing steadily stronger every day. The romantic, compassionate man that I had grown accustomed to trusting was evolving. He had become narcissistic, self-centered and greedy, interested only in himself and what others could do for him. He was temperamental and anxious most of the time, almost fearful, and it was completely out of character for him.

In bed at night, he demanded sexual fulfillment, whether I was willing or not, and intimacy instantly became a chore for me, no longer pleasurable like it had always been between us. He was, suddenly, forceful and selfish with his touch, doing only enough to benefit himself. His commands became unspoken, expected nightly routines that sickened every part of me. Georgio appeared to be discontented, always preoccupied with everything but me and I couldn't help but wonder where I was on his list.

"What's wrong with you, lately?" I had probed on several occasions.

"This is just the way I am," he egotistically told me, but it wasn't the Georgio I knew and I wasn't willing to accept it any longer. He had commanded me for the last time.

"Let me tell you the way I am," I barked. "I don't have the time or patience for your ego so why don't you just pack up your things and leave."

"You think you can just set me out on the street like trash?" He raged. "That's what I am to you now, trash? I've never done anything for you? I'm the best thing in your life but now you want to act like I don't matter? You want me to leave? Okay, that's fine. I'll leave." His bravado left me seething.

"Be out when I get back," I demanded and left my house with a slam of the door while he began gathering his clothes.

Fury masked my heartache as I recounted his callous words, his atypical actions from the previous weeks. Georgio had converted into someone that we both knew he wasn't and I struggled to understand how it had happened. What had caused the abrupt change in him that made him so inhuman and self-absorbed? I was hurt, and worse was that I was disappointed, not only in him for treating me so badly, but in myself for letting him, especially considering who I was. It was the one thing I had always sworn not to do, yet, I had taken abuse from both Georgio and Marco. It made my skin even thicker and I realized that I was better off alone.

I arrived home a couple of hours later to find Georgio and his belongings gone. All that remained of him were the memories of happier times. My heart dropped at the realization of his absence but I was convinced that it was for the best. My peace of mind was more important than the lonely nights that lay ahead of me. A scribbled note hung on the refrigerator.

Fran, I gotta be me. Sorry for the heartache I've caused. My love forever, Georgio. I crumbled up the small piece of paper, tossing it into the trash can and, with it, my devotion to the man I still loved.

Chapter 11

It was Sunday, a couple of weeks later, and I was finally beginning to heal my broken heart. After hundreds of tears and relentless self-pity, I was ready to pick myself up and move on with my life.

Like every week, I arrived at my parents' house for dinner with the family and everyone probing Georgio's whereabouts.

"We broke up," I casually announced as if his absence hadn't phased me.

"Oh, I'm so sorry, miele," my mother sympathetically responded while my father's face grew somber.

"What happened?" He probed, attentively putting down his fork.

"Nothing happened," I answered. "We just weren't moving in the same direction anymore. It's for the best and I feel good." It wasn't completely the truth but I felt it better to spare them the anguish. Disappointment plagued my father's face. He had grown to like and respect Georgio and clearly felt secure with me dating him. He trusted him to protect me the same way that he had always done.

Life, for me, continued in my lover's absence. Above all, I

was a Mafiosi and I could no longer allow my personal emotions to fog my goals. I was building an empire with a substantial crew of men working for me, all of them loyal and committed to one cause, the family. Each of us had more money than one could count but, moreover, was the respect that accompanied it. Lavish dinners and parties, elite cars and homes and expensive vacations, it was all part of the package. Sure, we had sold our souls to the devil but the rewards always overpowered the consequences. I found myself making valiant efforts to thwart off the guilt assaulting me from all of the dirt that I had done. I was donating money to charities, food banks and shelters, even the Catholic church. Whether it was my way of sharing my wealth or validating my culpability, giving just made me feel better. Besides, for us, there was never any shortage of money.

"Would you like to confess your sins to the Lord?" The Priest asked.

"Well, I would but God doesn't have all day to listen," was my lighthearted response. Life, I felt, had already dealt its fate to me and it was too late to reverse the damage. I was a mafia princess and nothing else.

One evening, my father called to invite me to dinner. "I have a business proposition for you," he said.

At the restaurant, lavishly decorated with fine linen and velvet, my father arose from his chair to greet me with a kiss on the cheek.

"Ah, splendido as always," he complimented.

"Well, grazie. I take after my handsome father."

The young waiter appeared with a bottle of the establishment's finest wine, merely because of who we were, a custom that we were used to.

"It's on the house", he commented.

"Frannie, I invited you here to talk about Georgio," my father finally admitted after several grueling minutes of small talk.

"I have nothing to say about him," I replied with exasperation. What was his infatuation with my former boyfriend?

"I want you to stop this foolishness and make amends with

him." I couldn't believe what I had just heard.

"You can't be serious, Papa," I said. Aside from the astonishment of him actually expecting me to do what he wanted was his deliberate neglect to even ask what Georgio may have done to me to cause our split.

"I'm very serious, yes," he responded with demanding eyes and an obvious motive in mind. "You will reconcile with him." His tone was insistent.

"That will not happen and, furthermore, I don't appreciate you commanding me like one of your consiglieres."

"You are my daughter and you will do as I say," he firmly insisted with his familiar intimidation but I refused to obey him. He could rule the rest of the world but no longer could he govern me, and my independence riled him.

"Why is this so important to you?" A hint of shame settled in his face and his head sank to the floor. "Papa?"

"Okay," he responded with an indignant sigh. "Georgio has been working for me." As gracefully as possible with the rage piercing my veins, I sat back in my chair, my glacial eyes stabbing my father's as jagged swords. His betrayal seemed unforgiveable and I wondered how we would ever recover. His remorseful eyes admitted his dishonor, his disloyalty to his own blood. "I agreed not to make him a consigliere as long as he was working with you but I owe him a huge debt for what his father did," my father tried to reason. "He's no longer working with you, right?"

He was right. Georgio no longer worked as my advisor and it wasn't only due to our breakup. It was his disrespect that had pushed me away. I would let no one dishonor me, even if it was my beloved father. In the commandments, his actions were cause for punishment, even as the Capo.

"If he's not removed by you, I will take this to the Commissione. It was, essentially, the Sicilian mafia's ruling body. Made up of top Cosa Nostra representatives, they set the standards and resolved disputes that arose between families. The problem was that my father was one of its officials. Still, he wasn't the only one and it took all fifteen of them to come to a consensus.

"Listen, we're family, so let's not bring this matter between us, Frannie," he told me. "You cut him loose so I really didn't see the harm. Now, I realize your anger over it so how about we just make a deal?"

"It better be a good one," I replied and I meant it.

After another half hour of negotiating with one another, my father and I agreed on a trade. Since Georgio knew the business of my clan, I was granted an advisor who knew well of my father's - Gino. The trade was fair enough for me, though I still refused to reconcile with Georgio, against my father's better judgment.

"How did you get to be so bull-headed?" He ribbed as we left the restaurant.

"I think it runs in the family," I responded with a devious grin and the pride gleamed in his eyes.

Later that evening, I rose up to answer a knock on the door. Georgio radiated the alluring smile that had always captivated me, dressed in his perfectly-fitted jeans and black leather jacket, his hair gelled. I couldn't deny my endless attraction to him. It had always remained regardless of the circumstances.

"Can I come in?" He asked in his rugged Italian tone and I found myself spellbound by the familiar aroma of his cologne as he breezed by me. I closed my eyes to savor it. Seeing him only reiterated how much I missed him in my life, and I fought the temptation to take him into my arms. I couldn't let him know that I still yearned for him so deeply because he had hurt me like no other.

"I heard about the meeting with your father today," he spoke with words of gentle sincerity. "I know I betrayed you and I'm sorry for that, but I also respect your authority in the family and want to thank you for not fighting mine."

"It wasn't an easy decision," I told him softly.

"This world has always been my life. I don't know anything else and I don't fit in anywhere else. It's where I belong."

"I know," I said and it was his loyalty which had aided in my decision. "You're actually good for my father, too." Georgio stared at me as if starving for my touch.

"Am I good for you?" I wasn't sure but he was always irresistible to me.

"No," I grinned and my words were pure but emotionally, physically, he was my breath. Slowly, he approached, his eyes drawn to mine until the feel of his hands on my shoulders sent explosions through my spine.

"You're my addiction, Francesca," he confessed, "what I crave. You're in my veins, someone I'm willing to die for. I bleed for you and breathe you in every day. You're my anguish and my euphoria."

"Stop talking!" I wanted to scream out to him, halting the poetic words of his magnetic lips that reeled in my tortured soul. Forbearing the man I desired felt impossible at that moment. I needed him desperately and, suddenly, all that had happened between us was nothing more than a faded memory, almost as if it had never happened at all. All we knew was that we needed each other.

The velvet lips that I swore I would die without softly caressed mine, releasing chills of ecstasy into my very soul, my entire body humming celebration within as if Heaven's angels were singing, and I melted in his arms once again. They were my haven, my home. His hands tingled every inch of my body as they journeyed on their mission and, as much as I needed to stop Georgio's affection, my weakness prevailed. He had become my infatuation, as well, and I discovered myself powerless to its demand. Passionately, on the floor of my living room, he ravished me like so many times before, my body crying out in bliss and pleading for more because I couldn't seem to get close enough. Explosion after explosion jilted my being with endless euphoric spasms until, eventually, reality made its comeback and I was left with only the consequences.

"That was amazing," Georgio remarked, and it was true, but it quickly became obvious to me that our encounter had given him false hope about our relationship as he spoke about our future together.

I made a swift escape to the bathroom, regretting my

actions. The heat of the moment had clouded my better judgment. My attraction to Georgio had gotten the best of me, causing my complete loss of self-control, but he needed to know that my future didn't include him. I was unsure of my ability to say goodbye but I had to because of the power struggle between us and because of our roles within the family.

"Fran, are you alright in there?" His voice echoed through the bathroom door and the moment of truth had arrived. I reluctantly made my way out.

"What is it?" He inquired when we sat on the couch. I took a deep breath and tried to find my words.

"I feel so much for you. I truly love you . . ."

"I love you, too," he intervened before I could complete my sentence, "more than I've ever loved any woman and, well, I'd be incredibly honored if you'd marry me." He presented a magnificent diamond ring that took my breath away. A proposal was the last thing I expected and it was a struggle to compose myself as I sat in amazement. Even as much as I loved and craved Georgio, accepting his proposal meant compromising my standard and potency.

"I can't and you know why," I replied despondently, already questioning my decision. "I'm sorry." He hung his head in disappointment, trying to recapture his pride. My rejection had rendered him wounded. In the discomforting silence that ensued, all I could do was console him in my arms.

"How can I go on without you?" I shared his sentiment, once again grieving my life without him. This was the finality of our relationship and those were the words that brought it to its end, the words that left me in agony with only the sweet memories of Georgio that I would carry with me forever.

I found myself trapped in an abyss of discord with myself for the decision I had made. It was a choice that was supposed to convey victory but it had, instead, rendered me vulnerable in my own security, miserable in my own sanity. I began to second-guess my choice. Maybe I needed Georgio more than I thought I did. Maybe he was more important to me than the title that I owned.

My mind was swimming with thoughts of my lover, memories that denied their escape. I recalled his invigorating smile, every line on his face, even the exact color of his eyes. I dreamed of feeling again what I had, enrapt in his heart. It seemed that no other man in the world could ever replace him. He was engraved in my soul. The death of our relationship tormented me but from it also came the desire to cultivate my empire.

I was transporting drugs and guns all over the world, from the United States and Britain throughout nearly all of Europe and in Asia. My contacts were people I trusted, spread throughout, who helped transport and receive the goods on private jets, yachts and trains, and they all loved the money. Drugs were big business and getting them to their destinations became easy since we had so much control. I had even started a few travel agencies to help cover it all. Everyone, it seemed, had a piece of the pie. The mafia organized and benefitted from everything and, what we didn't own, we still got a piece of in kickbacks. It was our entitlement. If someone wanted to own a business in our neighborhood, he had to pay the pizzo. It's true that money talks and, for us, it rejoiced. Everyone wanted to know us and be us. Our influence was unsurpassed and our cash flow limitless. We were both adored and feared, esteemed and respected, and we were everywhere. For some, the mafia was the tyrant but we were there to stay.

I started to notice an obvious void between my father and me. What began as indignation over my refusal to marry Georgio had quickly become bitterness. He no longer spoke to me as his daughter but as one of his colleagues and, much of the time, he made a vast effort to avoid me altogether. It was a hollowness that even my disengaged mother noticed. I was hurt but, moreover, baffled, left wondering what it was that had caused his sudden disregard of me. I wanted to ask him, talk about how to fix it but Mafiosi weren't exactly known for their heart to heart conversations. We agreed to meet for a drink at one of his establishments.

"What is this about?" He investigated.

"I want to know what's going on, why you've been

avoiding me," I replied. "Surely this isn't all because of Georgio."

"Get outta here," he responded in the typical mafia blow-off and it only fueled my suspicion.

"Why, Papa?" I demanded to know. He looked everywhere but at me in his discomfort, and the gauche silence was almost deafening.

"It's nothing," he finally spoke but I knew my father.

"You make me feel like I defied you in some way."

"You think you didn't?" He responded, and I wondered what sin I had committed.

"With Georgio?"

"With influence," he corrected icily. That was it. I had earned more dominance than he was comfortable with and, in his view, I had overstepped my boundaries. Though I had always been careful not to let my deals overlap my father's, he resented me. He was the mafia boss and I had no place on his level. It had never been my intention to challenge him in any way but he felt that I had.

"Papa, I never meant to . . ."

"It doesn't matter," he intervened, uninterested in my response. "Contempt is still betrayal and it's a fatal sin."

His words left me speechless. His status as the Capo forced a threat on his only child's life because there was no other choice. My father's bond with the mafia far exceeded his bond with me. They were his family first, taking precedence over even his wife and daughter, and this was an act of business. In an instant, I sped from heartbreak to fury, his words piercing me like the bullet he threatened. Rather than his blood, he saw me as they enemy, a predator of his position. It was the death of our relationship, as I knew it, and the grief was unbearable. Never had a loss been such torture for me because, unlike the rest, he was my father. I felt as though I had nothing left in the world. The only two things I knew in life were being a Mafiosi and being my father's daughter.

Marco had always played on my suffering and this was no exception. At my lowest point came his letter.

My Dearest Francesca, it began. *Every second here brings thoughts of you, like the sun amidst a storm. I dream of your smile and remember your eyes so vividly. In here, I realize my faults and battle my demons, hoping to come out a better man and earn another chance with you. My loyalty will forever stay with you as my love for you is greater than even for myself. I miss you and hope that you can forgive me. All my love, Marco.*

His poetic sentiments, even as trite as they may have seemed, never failed to pique my senses. Those were the words of adoration that women doted upon, a sweet symphony of the heart. Marco was the desire of every woman, attractive and debonair. There was a part of me that would always care for him as my first love but he could never be mine, not the way I needed him to be. Responding to his letter was dangerous so I left well enough alone, even with so much to say.

Chapter 12

Late at night the following week, the phone awoke me from my peaceful slumber.

"Frannie, I need to see you right away," my father's voice, abnormally frail and despondent, requested and panic invaded me.

"Now? Is everything alright?" My mind found a million reasons for the call, an accident, my mother, a death in the family.

"Come alone," a peculiar voice demanded.

"Who is this?" I probed with distrust. "What's going on?"

"You've got fifteen minutes."

So many scenarios illustrated my thoughts as I wondered what was happening. I pictured my father being held against his will, a gun to his head, and I wondered who the alien voice on the phone belonged to. My father's threat the week prior also left me wondering if the call was his ploy to scare me into submission. Maybe I was being set up for my own demise, but I needed to go in case my father truly was in trouble. The peculiarity of the call made me suspicious and uneasy. I realized that meeting with them could end my life but I couldn't ignore my father's pleas for help. His status made it possible and his fragile tone deemed it believable. No matter what the circumstance, I had to do as I was ordered and there was no more time to debate it. I had to take my chances. My heart beat against my chest as I wiped my sweating palms on my pants leg.

Packing two guns and a third in my car, I drove to the dock, five miles away. An eerie silence haunted the night with only a single light emitting a dim, orange hue over the bay, just like I had seen in the movies, and I knew nothing good ever came from those situations. I was plagued with anxiety, screaming at me to turn back, but I knew my duty. Stricken with fear and barely breathing, I made my way slowly to the dock where, at the edge, stood my father, his hands and feet bound with rope and weights and his eyes blinded with a cloth. My heart raced with horror and the hair on my arms came alive in the water's soft breeze as I feared who lurked in the dark shadows.

Darkness claimed my vision when I was blindfolded from behind and led a few feet to where I assumed was the edge of the dock, near my father. The only sound was my thumping heart, blaring in my ears, in the silence that pierced the darkness for several grueling minutes until a man finally spoke.

"A Capo and his daughter and, now that you're here, the situation is this. Both of you owe me and, well, one has to pay with his or her life, so let's see how loyal you are to each other," he said and I assumed that he must have been someone my father knew since his voice was unfamiliar to me. My father stood in silence, like me, dreading what would happen next. We didn't dare utter a word or ask any questions, though there were a thousand on my lips. It was an obvious plot that pitted the two of us against each other and, to me, it was outlandish. Neither of us would ever turn on the other. We were blood.

"Please, if this is about money . . ." my courageous father began but was abruptly shut down.

"This isn't about money," the strange man informed. "This is about loyalty and respect. Your money can't help you now. You took someone away from me so now, guess what? It's your turn. Which one will make the ultimate sacrifice for the other? You're family, right? Isn't this what family does for one another, especially a family as loyal as yours? Who's it going to be?"

I heard the soles of his dress shoes on the wooden dock, a slow pace back and forth as he spoke so confidently, and I wondered how many people were there with us. No one had even given any thought to our guns and it was never any secret that Mafiosi were always heavily armed. I had two that tempted me. Even blindfolded, my chances seemed good at hitting at least one guy, I thought, and even if they shot back, we were there to die anyway, it seemed. I felt that there was nothing to lose by taking the risk.

"Are you prepared to die for your father?" The man asked calmly asked me. I didn't need to ponder his question.

"Yes," I replied softly and certainly and, though I wasn't, I would have given my life if it meant saving his.

"Are you prepared to die for your daughter?" He then queried of my father and the silence deafened me. "Would you die for your daughter?" He repeated loudly.

"No," I heard him say and my body fell numb. His response rendered me aghast with disbelief. I couldn't absorb what I had just heard, my own father tossing me into the lion's den to save himself. My ears seared with pain over what little I truly meant to him and I wondered, at that moment, what my mother would think.

"Makes me glad you're not my father," the man commented, almost sympathetic to my wounded heart. "How about now, machile," he probed. "Still willing to give your life for this scum bag?" I had been diminished to nothing more than one of his employees, a person undeserving of his love and, even with a tortured soul, I loved my father.

"Yes," I answered hesitantly, prepared to die in the name of my father, even in spite of his refusal to die for me. My heart no longer feared but wailed with suffering. My soul shrieked in anguish from the wounds he initiated. It was the ultimate betrayal from one to another and the blood of our family had been, forever, tainted. I yearned to feel compassion from the man who had raised me and vowed his devotion to me. I wanted to hear his tears of appreciation for my sacrifice but all I heard was the water's gentle whispers.

"One," the countdown to my death had begun and my heart pounded harder than I ever knew it could. "Two." I saw my mother's generous eyes crying for me.

"God, forgive me," I prayed my last words and held my breath, prepared to be peppered with steel.

"Three," I heard the man say and that moment, my blindfold was removed and before my eyes, my father's life taken by a single bullet to the back. I witnessed, like slow motion, his decent into the icy waters and still, I yearned to leap in and save him. A mass pool of emotions floated through me upon his exit and I was left alone, unsure what to feel. I fell upon my weakened knees, staring into the water's depth, mourning my father's legacy, his memory, all that he was – and wasn't – to me. I thought of my mother's impending grief. These thieves had just stolen her life along with his.

"Francesca," I heard a familiar tone softly utter and I slowly turned to see fretful eyes on a satisfied face. Georgio peered, lovingly, into me as if awaiting my gratitude for his deed, the gun that had taken my father away still in hand, at his side. A tall, lanky man, only known to me by his voice, stood next to him. His expression spoke of nothing, serving only as an obedient soldier to my former flame, the man who had just murdered my father and, forever, altered my life.

"Why?" I tearfully probed his motive. "He loved you." It was true. My father had mentored Georgio as if he was his son, protecting and preening him.

"He didn't love *you*," he responded and I shook my head in mourning. Georgio lifted my face to wipe away my tears. "He was willing to let you die. He never loved you like I do, Fran. I'd die for you right now." He handed me his gun, the black steel warmed by his hand. I held the gun that had just taken my father's life. With disbelief and overwhelming sorrow, I recalled my love for Georgio, the intensity that it held in the beginning, the way that he once meant more to me than anyone else in the entire world. I was lost in desperation, broken from deceit and, in an instant, without another thought or emotion, I lifted his gun with trembling hands and fired into both him and his partner until they lay motionless on the dock. I knew, and they did, that they had to die for what they had done. Under its commandments, the wage for the murder of a Capo was death.

I tried to feel something, anything, but the shock of it all had rendered me numb. Fatigue had taken control as I awaited two of my consigliers, whom I had called to meet me there.

"You look like you've just seen a ghost," one remarked when they arrived.

"I have," I responded with a void stare. "They killed the Capo, Lorenzo." It was how I referred to my father around others.

I led them to the bodies on the dock and their job was to dispose of them. "We need to get him out of there," I spoke of my father. I wanted his body recovered from the bay for a proper burial. It wasn't out of respect for him but for the dignity of my mother. I couldn't have her know the truth about his death.

Still reeling from the night's events, I drove home to collect my thoughts before talking to my mother. I was trapped inside of an unbreakable trance, unable to wrap my mind around the night's events. The two men that I loved most in the world were gone, murdered, and it had destroyed me inside. One had died because he didn't love me enough and the other because he loved me too much. Georgio had made a final profession of his love for me in the most profound way possible, and then there was my father, a man who would have given his life for any one of his consiglieres on any given day but not for me. The thought of it tormented me and would forever. Our rocky relationship could never be mended, but I had to forgive so that it didn't eat me up inside. Lorenzo Mazonelli was still my father and his legacy still lived in me.

I knew that my mother would surely be crippled by the loss of her husband, a burden that would fall on me, and I needed to compose myself before breaking the news to her. He was the only man that she had ever loved, and they had been together for many years. She was dependent on my father for so many things and the loss of him, I knew, would leave her heartbroken and desolate. The pain of the Capo's death would be felt by so many that were close to him but there was no vengeance to be had. It was a huge loss that left everything in question.

The night had rendered me restless with my thoughts as I drove to my mother's majestic brick home, where she had shared so many memories with my father. My heart ached with the thought of breaking the news to her. It was the absolute last thing in the world that I wanted to do as I searched my mind for the right words, the right way, to tell her that her husband, my father, was dead.

"Are you alright, familiare? You look exhausted," she said with a caress of my cheek.

"No, Mama, I'm not alright," I tearfully confessed. "I have some bad news." She sat down with her hands in mine and, with a deep breath, I tried to muster up my courage. "I don't quite know how to tell you this, but Papa's gone, Mama." Confusion struck her face.

"Gone? What? Gone where?" I stared into her wounded eyes to try again.

"He died, Mama," I rephrased, softly, and she sat, idly, attempting to absorb my words. "I'm so sorry." Her dark eyes slowly scanned her surroundings as if she was stunned and speechless until, eventually, she peered at me once again.

"How?" She probed, still unable to cry from the shock of it all. I had spent hours thinking up a scenario that was both believable and would leave my parents with dignity while thwarting off any suspicion.

"He had a heart attack," I fabricated and hoped that she never learned the truth. "He was night fishing in the bay." My story, somehow, brought a sense of peace to her that, at least her husband had died doing something that he enjoyed.

Slowly, she arose and walked over to the colossal bay window that overlooked their cherished vineyard, and I sat in silence as she stared into the outside world. My news had shattered her life, as she knew it, and I was sure that she questioned her future without my father. He was all she had known since they were fifteen years old and, now, she was forced to go on without him. Her entire world had changed in an instant and I worried about her sanity. Quietly, I approached and put my hand on her shoulder.

"It's going to be okay," I assured her. "We'll get through this."

She turned and looked at me, as an abused child, tears silently flowing down her cheeks, and I embraced her. It wasn't until then that I wept over the death of my father and, still, I believe it was more for her that I grieved. Always, he had held such a fervent presence in our lives and neither of us really knew how to face the world without him. In one another's arms we cried, mourning our loss and lending strength to each other.

"Your father was a great man," she said, and I understood that she didn't know his life the way that I did and I didn't know it the way that she did. Each of us saw separate sides of him as if he lived two different lives. In many ways, he did. "What am I going to do? I'm really going to miss him." Her sentiment tortured my heart. I never could bear to see my mother hurting.

"I'm going to miss him, too, Mama," I told her, "but we'll get through this together."

Word of my father's death spread rapidly, triggering phone calls, gifts of sympathy and visitors that were increasing in numbers, and it seemed to help my mother. It also gave me a small window of time to call Gino.

"Is everything taken care of?" I asked him.

"Yes, it's being done as we speak," he replied confidently. As crazy as it might sound, my father had taken ownership of two funeral homes.

"And did you find what we were looking for?" It was understood that I was referring to my father's body being retrieved from the water.

"We do have it," was his response, short and to the point, like I preferred. "Everything is fine and I'll see you shortly." As crazy as it might sound, my father had taken ownership of two funeral homes.

I returned to a house full of family, friends and neighbors, all bearing food, as Sicilians did no matter what the occasion, offering their condolences to my mother and me over the loss of my father. They shared their own memories of him and stories of their experiences with him throughout the years.

"Francesca, miele, I haven't seen your mother in a while," my cousin, Theresa, said to me a couple hours later. "I am worried about her."

"I know where she is," I told her and I went out into the vineyard.

"Are you doing okay, Mama?" I asked as she strolled, leisurely, through the rows.

"I'm fine," she answered, turning to me with a faint smile, "just needed a little breather." She inhaled deeply with memories of her husband in her mind. "Your father really loved this vineyard. We planted it when you were just a baby. Making these old grapes into wine was such a passion of his", she reminisced as we walked. "How am I going to keep up with it now?" Once again, she erupted into tears as I consoled her in my arms and, when the tears stopped, she glared up to the Heavens as if in search of him. "It's just like you, Lorenzo, to leave me to this, all on my own," she commented as I patiently listened to her. She continued on as if I wasn't there. "You were always somewhere else, never at home but always with your so-called 'family' or those other women, always off, fulfilling your own needs. I had needs, too, you know," she spoke and her words left me stunned. Maybe my mother knew more about his life than I thought. "I gave you my all." Her dedication and loyalty to him overshadowed even his betrayal of her. She did know his world, his part in the Cosa Nostra, but she had chosen it to be his world, alone. She had made my father and me hers, and we were all that mattered to her.

My father's wake was packed with people, from Mafiosi to ministers. Politicians and judges, police all came to pay respect. It seemed the entire town had come to say goodbye to the man who had so greatly influenced their lives, whether good or bad. Some were strangers to his world, merely stopping for a glance at Sicily's most powerful and notorious celebrity.

I stared down at my father's lifeless body in the casket, still intimidated by his domination, and I felt that he would open his eyes, at any moment, rising up with his brawny hands on my throat for causing his death, the eerie chill in my veins forcing a step backward to put me out of his reach. Even in view of a corpse, I didn't see him as dead. Death could never overtake a man so powerful, I thought, but, somehow, it had and life would be altered. Forever, I would carry the curse of his murder, never knowing freedom from it. His voice, his image, his disappointment would haunt me for all of my days and, already, I felt his presence vividly, almost as if he was right behind me.

My mother placed her hand gently over his with a proud smile, and I was amazed by her unconditional love and devotion. It was a trait that I hadn't inherited. With fragility, she leaned in for a final kiss on his forehead.

"Kiss your father goodbye, machile," she said but fear tormented me.

"I already have," I fibbed, unwilling to obey her morbid suggestion.

I think it was difficult for everyone to grasp that the mob boss was really gone. He had always emanated a mortality that superseded even death. No one could accept the permanence of his absence. We were a kingdom without its ruler, all unsure how to cope on our own.

The sudden outburst of whispers in the room drew my attention to the entryway where, in a revealing, form-fitting teal dress, stood a saucy, well-endowed redhead, overloaded with makeup and jewelry and reeking with perfume. We all knew her, not by name, but as my father's mistress. I was infuriated by her audacity and blatant disrespect for my mother, who stood, wide-eyed, with disbelief as the room awaited a reaction.

"Stay here, Ma," I said and hurried over to the woman.

"Oh, darling, I am so sorry," she uttered empathetically in

her upper class intonation. "Your father thought the world of you." She spoke as if she knew him better than anyone. Maybe she did, given the circumstances, but her presence was unwelcome as far as anyone was concerned.

"This is extremely inappropriate and disrespectful to his family so you need to leave right now," I told her before she could penetrate the room any further.

"I have the same right to be here as everyone else," she boldly responded as if I had no authority. Their affair of twenty years, she felt, granted her the privilege to be there.

"At the risk of making an unwanted scene at this wake, I'm going to ask you, once again, and only once again, to leave or I'll have you escorted out in front of everyone here. Passato?" She glared at me with eyes of fire, piercing lasers ready to raze furiously through me, and I stared back with the same vengeance, daring her to make a move. Over my shoulder, his lover glanced at the casket that gracefully held my father and, with a sigh of defeat, she turned to leave. Humiliation plagued my mother as those around us struggled not to stare.

"It's alright, Mama," I consoled with my arm around her shoulder as the shame of the situation clouded her. I felt bad for her, sorry for her, having to live in the shadow of my father's mistress for so many years, only to see her show up at his wake for everyone to question and gossip about. It eroded her integrity.

The air was frosty as, later, we sat at my father's graveside, listening to the hymn of departure being gloriously belted out from a chorus member of our Catholic church. For me, it spoke of the true finale of a life treasured by so many, and it was the saddest part of the wake. The opened earth made his death genuine and everlasting. Now it was real and I suffered through my tears, paying my utmost respect to my father, whether deserving or not. I cherished him for my life and its lessons and, above all, I appreciated him for my mother's fulfillment. Truly, I would miss him.

With the loss, I hadn't allowed myself time to grieve for Georgio. I had taken the life of the man I loved but he had taken my father's. Had it truly been for me, or rather his own personal vendetta? I would never know the answer and, meanwhile, the two men who meant the most to me in the world were gone forever. The reasons no longer mattered. I cried out for them, wailed over their absence, and it suffocated me to know that I could never see them again. They remained as no more than mere memories in my heart.

I now knew what it was to take a life. I had taken Georgio's, and with the overwhelming grief came a strange overtone of peace because I had gotten vengeance for the death of my father. So long it was that I wondered how Mafiosi could kill someone so easily, without even a second thought, without an ounce of remorse. Always, I had associated it with the exhilaration of supremacy but it didn't feel that way. It felt almost meaningless, and so much of me regretted my actions.

Chapter 13

My father's death left the "family" void of its Capo and a wealth of anger toward the men I had killed. They yearned for revenge that couldn't be had, while mourning the man who meant everything to them. No one really knew what to do next. None of us knew how to move on without him.

The vacancy needed to be filled in the cosca. There remained an empty seat for a Capo and the question of who would fill it. A meeting among key advisors and Commissione members was held to determine who would assume my father's esteemed position, both on the Board and within the family. As much as we all mourned, it had to be done quickly.

"Ordinarily, in a situation such as this, the Sotto Capo would assume the responsibilities of the Capo," one Commissione leader informed the group and a telltale grin crossed Vinny's proud face. "However, in this particular circumstance, Lorenzo left specific instructions."

The heads of the family began to turn, eyes peering at others, questioning the future. No mob boss had ever done that, leaving instructions for what was to ensue in the event of his death.

It had left us all swimming in bewilderment, none of us knowing what to think.

Commissione and Cosca, his letter began. *It has been my esteemed pleasure working with all of you and especially those of you in the family. With my passing comes the burden of replacing me and, understanding the target that my position has made me, this appointment has played over in my mind a hundred times. At the risk of offending my Sotto Capo (whomever it may be at the time of my exit), my wish and my order is for "Petey" to assume my role in the family.*

The puzzled faces scanned the room to see who it was that would claim such an esteemed title as the mob boss.

"Petey?" They probed. "Who's Petey?" There was no one they knew by that name and it left everyone stumped, everyone but me. I dropped my head as the tears invaded my eyes. My father did care after all. He had faith in me after all, and it meant everything.

"It's me," I confessed awkwardly and tearfully. Petey was the nickname I had been given by my father as a young child, the result of an overplayed joke about how he had hoped for a boy.

My admission evoked the baffled stares of every person there, each of them surely wondering why, or how, a woman could be elected. I found myself questioning the same. Women were never intended to be active members of the mafia, and especially not a capo. It just wasn't acceptable or even heard of. Vinny appeared defeated and cross. The title that he had worked so hard to earn had just been stolen from him as if his years of loyalty meant nothing to my father. We all knew that it was rightfully he who deserved to lead the cosca. My father, the same man who, at his end, had betrayed his only child, had recognized my dream but knew that the title could never be mine unless he bequeathed it.

"I sit here, truly as stunned as the rest of you, over the capo's decision," I said to the table of onlookers, "so I vote to respectfully relinquish the role and its duties to Vinny, as it has always been the underboss who assumes this role, and he is more deserving."

"Please understand, Francesca, that it is the *Commissione's* position to inform you that, although it does, reverently, honor your inclination, it is also its duty to remind that refusing the appointment is duly considered discourteous to the organization." I did want to accept it but the title was Vinny's to relish and I would have to take my chances. Vinny stared at me with admiration on his face, seemingly astounded by my willingness to step aside.

"I'm grateful, but it's my preference to resume my duties as the Sotto," he replied to the group and, though I knew he wasn't certain of his decision, he nodded at me as if he was. It spoke of his faith in me and I was proud.

"Alright, then, any objections to this conclusion?" None surfaced but I was sure there were a discontented several, holding their tongues while knowing better than to oppose. For that reason, I would be forced to watch my back. Greed was no stranger to power and betrayal was always the companion of envy. I knew that many of them would struggle to obey the commands of a woman. Some would rather serve their enemies. With nothing else said, the decision was final. I was the new mob boss and the first woman, ever, to become one. Already, I had made history but respect was what I needed to obtain. There may not have been any open opposition but I wasn't naïve enough to assume that everyone approved. I knew better. None of them were above whacking a woman the same way as they would a man, even if it was a sin of the commandments. Dominance was their priority and I, for the moment at least, was the one who possessed it.

Since I had been, somewhat, separate from my father's dealings, I had to be brought up to date on the current activities, as an assistant manager being promoted to a manager in a company would be. It was what I had dreamed of my entire life and I was up to the challenge.

Word of a new Capo spread rapidly, even to Marco in prison.

"He is grieving the deaths of your father and Georgio," Mario, who remained in frequent contact with him, told me, "but he wants me to congratulate you."

It came to my attention that Marco still played a major role in the cosca, giving orders from behind bars, which I had never been aware of. He remained very tuned in on our activities which I found discomforting. Every piece of information that he had presented a greater risk to the family, and I suddenly understood my father's reservations about him after his arrest. As long as he was incarcerated, he couldn't play an active role in the organization, as far as I was concerned.

"He takes care of things on the inside," Mario informed me. Working with other Mafiosi who were incarcerated, Marco had established his own dealings, offering protection, selling drugs, whatever was able to make him money, most of which was being filtered back to us. He was, seemingly, even more powerful behind bars than he was on the street and he used it to benefit the family. We knew everything that went on or was about to. In prison, one's business was never secret. The family had even managed to have some of its enemies whacked on the inside, pentiti and such. Whether right or wrong, Marco still played an intricate part within the organization and, while risky, my father was smart for doing it. For me, the risk outweighed the benefit. One wrong move on his part could easily disintegrate the family. It was a chance that I just wasn't willing to take.

Needless to say and, as I suspected, Marco didn't take the news well and assumed that he was being undeservingly dismissed.

"I should be commended for my work in here and, instead, I'm being disrespected," he told Mario. Marco would be rewarded for his silence and cooperation, surely, but not until he was freed. I had to protect the family and its assets. It was a business decision.

In the wake of my father's death, my mother, still grieving and fragile, had become clingy, constantly wanting me with her. She had never really been alone and didn't know quite how to cope. She spoke, endlessly, about what a wonderful and devoted family man he was, and I wondered where her sentiments came from. The man I knew was never rueful about tossing her aside for "business" or excursions with his fiery haired mistress. He was a man who, for the most part, ignored his wife except for the occasional outing. Since I had grown up, even his vacations were spent with his mistress. Still, they had shared their lives together and my mother didn't know anything else. She had chosen to turn a blind eye to my father's transgressions and forgiven him completely. All that she had ever really had in the world was him and me and, since half of that was gone, she clung to the remnants. As much as I adored this woman who gave me life, her constant need for me was exhausting. I found that I had no time for anything other than her, and there was business to be done. It was then that I truly understood my father's need to be away from the house and our family.

"Mama, I think you should get away for a little while, take a vacation to get your mind off of things." I admit that the suggestion was just as self-serving as it was for her. "You haven't been on a vacation in years."

"I can't do that," she replied. "What about the restaurant?" I assured her that I would take care of everything and, with a little additional insistence, my mother agreed to go on a three-week cruise. Finally, I could breathe again.

With her gone, I could get back to business and, after getting a temporary manager in my mother's restaurant, my first priority was a judge who had been crusading against us. Judge Catorro, from the time of his election, had been strong opposition for the Cosa Nostra, leading the fight to convict key members and shut down its activities with his anti-mafia campaigns. He was fearless in his fight against corruption and, truly, about the only one who couldn't be paid off by us. We were practically the theme to his campaign, his fight to be elected. Fortunately for us, there were more people on our side than on his. After several meetings, the Commissione decided to fight back. I was about to order my first hit on another human being and my conscience was in a fight with my authority.

I gathered together my top Advisors – Gino, Leo, Angelo, Carmine and Mario – all who had been the same to my father.

"The Commissione has granted approval to take out Catorro," I informed them, straight-faced.

"Car bomb?" Angelo suggested.

"I think we need to send a message here," I said. "He has plenty of advocates, enlisted a lot of key officials, and I want them to know that it's not a smart move."

"What are you thinking?" Carmine probed.

"Cut out his tongue," I commanded coldly, shocked at my own words. "Take his eyes out, too. Let them know we mean business." I couldn't believe what I was saying, words so brutal, but no Mafiosi had ever let compassion stand in the way of business. I had to be tough. I had to be numb and play the role that I had inherited, even if it did test my conscience.

When I heard, the next day, that my orders had been promptly carried out, contrition mixed with supremacy vibrated through me like electricity in my veins. It was superiority at its best, an elation that I had never felt before, combined with a tremendous sense of remorse. I had taken someone's husband and father away. Still, it consumed me with the rush of glory that I had craved all of my life. I was invincible and, suddenly, nothing was a crime. My decisions were bold, but never reckless, and everything I did I felt was warranted.

It was one of our nights at Nico's, a mob-infiltrated bar on the outskirts of town, when Gino approached me privately.

"Salute," he greeted me in a toast. "How ya doin' these days?" He asked.

"You mean without my father?" It was the first time I had ever referred to him as anything other than the Capo to anyone in the family and it felt strange.

"Yeah," he replied. "You had a big weight put on your shoulders but you seem to be handling things well." I was thrilled to receive his approval, almost as if receiving my father's.

"Is there any other way?" Standing strong was my only option.

"Not in our world," he said. "I've known you since you were a baby, Fran, and your father even longer. He was a great man, like a brother to me, so if there's anything you need . . ." It was his way of letting me know he had my back and that I was doing an okay job as the new boss.

"I know, Gino, thanks. You're the only person I can still trust." It was true, Gino had been family to me in all of my years and I knew that he would never betray me, even if my own father had.

"How about a handsome stripper for the night?" I joked.

"Eh, that could be arranged," he chuckled. "Speaking of that, though, I do have a charming young gentleman I'd like you to meet."

"You want to set me up on a date?" I wasn't sure that I was ready. "Does he know who I am?" As the capo, I had to be conscious of befriending people. My position made my life a dangerous business rather than personal pleasures. I had to be careful who I associated with and to what extent. No one could be trusted.

"Actually, he's new in town and probably the only one who doesn't know who you are," Gino replied with a snicker. I was hesitant but I did have to admit my loneliness and need for companionship. "Give it a try. It's just dinner, not commitment, and it might even spice up your life a little," he added with a sly wink.

"Well, I could definitely use that," I grinned.

As a capo, no one could introduce himself to me. Only third party introductions by a high-ranking advisor were permitted. Anyone who wanted to speak to me had to go through them. For the purpose of disguising my title, I was willing to make an exception. A blind date would be awkward enough without a third wheel hanging around.

I agreed to meet Emilio at Bello Palazzo, an elegant Italian establishment across town. It was my first blind date and I was already thinking of a way out of it as I reluctantly clad myself in a sensible, yet sexy, black dress. Going on a date made me defiant of every rule as a capo, I felt. Underneath was my gun, strapped to my thigh. Even on a date, I had to be protected. My nerves were getting the best of me as I wondered what I was getting myself into, and there were several times that I almost turned my car around on my way there. Dating just wasn't the priority at that time.

"It's just dinner, not commitment." I replayed Gino's words in my mind as I took a deep breath. "I should be focused on business, not this."

Inside, I was escorted to a cozy, candlelit table for two where, to my surprise, an average-sized, blond-haired man in his thirties rose from his velvet chair with a single red rose. He wasn't of the Sicilian breed that I was used to but rather an American with a strong Italian accent. Neatly dressed in a dark suit, he appeared suave as he offered me the rose with a welcoming smile.

"Thank you," I responded softly as he gracefully pulled out my chair. It wasn't an instant attraction for me but I had to admit that I welcomed his charm.

"Thank you for so generously joining me this evening."

"It's obvious that you're not Sicilian. I understand you've just moved here?"

"Good observation and yes," he replied. "I'm from the U.S., Brooklyn, New York, to be exact. I moved here on business, just last month, so I'm still fumbling my way around town. He explained that he was an art dealer and entrepreneur. "I dabble in a number of things."

"Interesting," I responded. "Me too."

"Really? What do you do?"

"Good question," I thought while fumbling for the answer. It was one I had never before had to explain. Everyone around town knew or, at least, highly suspected. I remembered what my father had once told me. "I'm in management," I echoed his words to my inquisitive companion, "and I own a few properties." It was all that needed to be said and I hoped that he wouldn't probe any further. "Blind dates are new to me and, just to be honest, I'm not a fan of them, no offense," I uttered in an attempt to change the subject. I found myself sipping champagne much faster than usual, just to calm my nerves.

"It's the second for me," Emilio replied. "My first blind date was a disaster from the start. She was nothing like she had claimed to be. I guess that's why they call it 'blind', eh?"

"I really don't date much at all," I remarked. "I'm sort of married to my job so it makes it tough." Maybe I should have felt guilty about my lies but I couldn't reveal my true identity, especially to a stranger. Secrecy, it was the story of my life and I had become quite a pro at it.

The date proceeded well and I liked Emilio, but disguising the truth about myself proved more difficult than I had imagined. I realized that a Mafiosi was probably a better fit for me. I needed someone who understood and accepted my lifestyle, but my title would only complicate my chances. It seemed that my only real option was to be alone and, after what I'd already been through with Marco and Georgio, I didn't need any more complications.

Chapter 14

With my mother out of town, I was taking care of her house and bills in her absence while also checking on the restaurant. A letter from her attorney caught my attention, immediately. I opened it to discover that my father's mistress was demanding money and assets that he had promised her.

"Is this some kind of joke?" I asked in the attorney's office the following day.

"No, I'm afraid it isn't," Luigi replied with a deep breath. "She wants twenty-eight thousand lira and the villa that Lorenzo set her up in."

"She won't get any of it." I was appalled at her efforts to stake claim on my father's assets and further torture my family.

"Well, maybe," Luigi responded. "The villa was leased by your father but also lists her name. The lira he allegedly promised is nothing more than a verbal agreement which we may be able to fight. Still, the best thing, if you want to keep this out of the media, is to try and negotiate a deal with her," he advised. "Maybe let her keep the villa, which she may be entitled to anyway, but refuse any payments." She had been my father's girlfriend for twenty years and a part of me knew that she was entitled to some part of him, even as wrong as it was to my mother and me. The attorney was right.

"You know that my mother won't cope well with this," I told him.

"All the more reason to resolve it now so that she won't know," he spoke, nonchalantly.

With all that my mother had already been through, I couldn't allow any further strain on her. It was a matter that needed to be taken care of before she even learned of it. There was no question that I needed to take things into my own hands.

When his lover refused to let me in the door, I shot through the locks with her screams in the background.

"Shut up and listen," I commanded, holding her violently against the wall with my hand around her throat. "What you're doing isn't very smart because you're messing with my family, and I'm sure you know what that means. You've already taken enough from my mother and, frankly, I've been more tolerant than I should have, already, so now it's time to call this thing off before you get hurt, capish?" I released her from my grip.

"Your father promised me these things," she whined like a child in a tantrum with her trembling, fearful voice. "I deserve them." In a rage, I grabbed the red-haired woman by the throat, shoving her violently against the wall again with my gun to her face, and the potency of her strong-smelling perfume appalled me.

"I think you know what I'm capable of," I reminded her. "You know who I am."

"Okay," she surrendered in fear of the consequences. "I'll drop it. Just please don't kill me," she pleaded with fiery red-stained lips. "Please."

"It better be history by tomorrow because, if I have to come back here, you'll disappear!"

By the commandments of the organization, women were not to be involved in mafia dealings or injured in any way, so killing, or even hurting, the woman was out of the question but she didn't know that. In my wrath, I had already pushed the limits by putting my hands on her like I had. My threat needed to be enough and I knew that it would be. No one was ever courageous enough to challenge a Mafiosi, especially where family or money was concerned.

I suppose I was an exception to the rule. Women had never been permitted into the mafia until I pioneered the change. My father had seen it in my eyes, the passion for it all. "The eyes of a panther," he used to call them, striking and sly, a fierce predator. There I was, the first mafia queen, a royal matriarch determined to protect her clan. I was young and, though still a bit naïve, my heart was of a lion, my ambition of a soldier. I was my father's daughter. Still, I was learning as I lived it.

We gathered daily, my consiglieres and me, at the same little bar on the outskirts of town, to discuss business – who owed money, who needed money, what was being transported in and out of Sicily – that kind of thing. Each of us oversaw the activities of others, like managers of a team. I was informed of everything that went on and no decisions were made without my approval. There were a number of families in the organization and all had to co-exist respectfully.

"Scampisi owes on the car dealerships," Leo announced during one of our meetings. "He's been avoiding us."

"Renato, down at the marina, wants sixty thousand lira for the shipment," Angelo added.

"How much does Scampisi owe us?" I queried.

"Three months with interest," Leo replied.

"Yeah, that's too long. Someone has to be running the dealerships so he isn't far away. Let's find him and remind him that we need the money, plus interest, by next week. We start taking out his inventory if he doesn't come up with it. As far as Renato goes, you tell him he knows the deal. It's fifty thousand for the shipment. Either he wants the cut or he doesn't and, if he wants to play games, so can we.

"Sure thing, Boss," Angelo agreed.

"Has anyone been by to see Giusino?" I asked. "The election is coming up and I want to make sure that he gets the votes. Carmine, find out what he needs."

Mayor Giusino had taken mafia payouts for years to help fund his campaigns, along with his prostitute and cocaine addictions. He was a close associate of the organization, catering to our needs while turning the other cheek, so to speak, and it was imperative for us to work together. The mafia strategically funded numerous key officials throughout Sicily who could aid in the advancement of its activities. Corrupt police and political figures were a dime a dozen, and each one of them had his hand extended to us. It was an easy system. We kept the right people in the right places.

I pulled Angelo aside and handed him twenty thousand lira.

"Take this to the bayside deli, downtown, and leave it with Sergio. Tell him that an assistant to Giusino will be coming for it." The money was an additional "campaign contribution" in exchange for Marco being released from prison. I had discovered, early on, that lira could buy anyone, and I used it to my best advantages.

My date with Emilio had been uneventful dining accompanied by casual conversation. Truth be told, I had no interest in seeing him again. He, however, had already become smitten with me, and I soon found myself barraged with gifts – flowers, candy, fine art, even jewelry – continuously being delivered to my door. Every exquisite surprise rendered me speechless with its sentiment but it was quickly overwhelming me.

"Grazie, so much, for all of the gifts, Emilio," I told him on the phone, "but I think you've got the wrong idea about us."

"I really enjoy your company, Francesca, and I'd like to see you again." I explained to him, as bluntly as I could without getting boorish, that I wasn't interested in pursuing anything further with him. "I think I can change your mind," he continued, beaming with confidence. I could see a future of endless stalking and high hopes from him so I needed to be clear.

"Do you know who I am, Emilio?" I was hoping that my identity would deter his mission. "I'm a pretty powerful person around here." He roared in amusement.

"Alright," he ribbed in typical "tough guy" fashion.

"It's not a joke," I affirmed with a poker face. "I can't really focus on a relationship, or even dating. My life is business." Emilio may not have understood the Cosa Nostra but I was sure of his familiarity in the mafia of New York, and they weren't much different from us so I hoped that he understood.

A few days later, a familiar knock came to my door. I knew, immediately, that it was Marco, and it brought back my smile.

"How are you?" I greeted him as he embraced me tightly. The proverbial blend of aftershave and his cologne captivated me like it always had before. He looked the same but healthier, more alive.

"I'm great," he answered and released me. "You are breathtaking, as always." He expressed his sympathy over the loss of my father and over his longtime friend, Georgio. "We never want to do these things," he commented as if he knew what had happened. I was sure that he did know but I refused to confess to being behind it.

"You look good, Marco," I complimented, and it was the truth.

"I've missed you so much, Fran," he said with a loving gaze. "Not a day has gone by that I haven't thought about you." Once again, he invoked my smile.

"I thought of you, too," I admitted. Marco seemed, somehow, different since his release from prison. He appeared sincere, mature, the opposite of the egotistical self-indulger that went in. I wanted to tell him how sorry I was for hurting him and how much I had truly missed him. I wanted him to notice how alone I felt in the world and how much I needed him as my confidante, but how could I when I had left him for his friend? I refrained. Besides, in my business, feelings were suppressed, not discussed. I couldn't allow my feelings as a woman to interfere.

"I know that I'm out of prison because of you," he said.

"Yes, but you did right by us and that earned your rank," I told him. "I know that you were still working in there."

Marco and I talked for more than two hours about our lives

and goals. He spoke of his experiences in prison but, for a Mafiosi, incarceration was just the chance we took. It was part of the game. I talked to him about the loss of my father, though I never admitted the truth.

"He was different before his death," I said, but I never spoke of his betrayal of me. Never would I disrespect his name, regardless of the circumstances.

"Francesca," Marco said with serious eyes, "I'm divorcing my wife." His words rattled every ounce of me. His marriage had been the only obstacle between us, a barricade that I assumed would never crumble. "I had nothing but time to think in prison so I did a lot of soul searching, and I realized that I'm married to the wrong woman. I recognized that I haven't loved her for years. We just kind of co-exist, like roommates, I guess because it's what we're supposed to do as husband and wife."

I understood, but a divorce wasn't acceptable or permitted in our world. Even as much as wives were kept out of our business as much as possible, they still knew too much. The family couldn't have a scorned and vengeful woman on our hands.

"You know that you can't divorce her, Marco," I reminded him, even though I may have wanted it as much as he did, at least at one time.

"She's not a pentiti. She won't squeal," he assured. "Besides, she knows nothing." Even if it were true, it meant very little. Marco needed to stay married and appease his wife, until death, and there was no alternative.

My mother was due to return home the following day, and I drove to the airport to pick her up. She appeared rejuvenated and relaxed.

"Ah, Mama," I greeted with a hug and kiss on her cheeks. "How was your trip?"

"Ciao, Miele. It was amazing," she answered joyfully. "I almost feel like a new woman." She asked about what had been going on but I didn't dare speak of the lawsuit filed by my father's mistress. Since I had threatened her, it had been promptly withdrawn anyway so I figured what my mother didn't know wouldn't hurt her. I drove her to her house and unloaded her mountain of luggage onto her bedroom floor.

"This house is still so empty without your father here," she remarked as she peered around the room, almost as if in search of him. "It's so quiet."

"Maybe you should just sell the house and buy something a little smaller," I suggested to her. "You don't really need a house this big anymore."

"Ah, no, I couldn't. There's a lifetime of memories here that I couldn't bear to part with." As quickly as it began, the conversation was ended by her and a new subject brought about. "I got you something overseas. You're going to adore it." From one of her garment bags she retrieved a mink coat, authentic and plush, that astounded my vision. Even with all the money and possessions that I had, never had I owned the mink coat that I'd always wanted.

"Oh, Mama, it's stupendo," I told her with awestruck eyes. I swore that it was the softest fur I had ever felt in my life.

"Try it on," she said with a proud grin. It felt like putting on a magic cloak. The coat seemed to transform me.

"You shouldn't have done this but I absolutely love it," I told her and hugged her tightly with appreciation.

The gifts from Emilio also continued, even in spite of my attempt to rid myself of him. Still, he showered me with flowers, candy and expensive offerings but I wasn't impressed. It seemed that the more I refused his attention, the more of it he gave. His actions finally led me back to Gino.

"Please make him stop this," I insisted.

"Emilio's a good man," he responded. "You don't like him?"

"He's just not my type but he doesn't seem to get it."

"Maybe you just got off on the wrong foot. Why don't you just give him one more chance?"

"I'm not interested."

"He must really be trying to impress you to go to this extreme," Gino remarked. "Just give the poor chump a break."

"No, Gino, you give me a break and get him off my back,

got it?"

"Enough said," he agreed.

Chapter 15

It was business, as usual, until it came to light that two families had become engrossed in a fierce dispute over property. Members of both clans each claimed ownership of a cluster of warehouses on the edge of town, and the argument had escalated to the extreme of death threats.

"Bianchi wants permission to take out Guiseppe," Mario informed me. In the underworld, people had been killed for a lot less. Mafiosi were always very protective of their possessions. Guiseppe was asking for my permission and I could have given it without any question.

"I want to see them both," I requested, and it was Mario's task to bring them in. By the day's end, he presented only one. "Where's Bianchi?" I asked the men, and Mario peered down at the other.

"Dead," was Guiseppe's response. His face fell flushed with the shame of his betrayal and fear of the consequences. I glared, sternly, at him.

"You disobeyed the commandment," I told him. "You had

no authority to carry out a killing." It was the first time that anyone had ever defied me, and I was unsure of what to do. It was the difference between my father and me. I was subtly changing the way that the cosa nostra operated, not intentionally, of course. It was simply a product of my upbringing and it made me realize why Mafiosi didn't want women involved in their activities.

"I'm sorry, Boss," he uttered, remorsefully, "but he was out to get me first so I felt it had to be done, in defense. It was a quick decision."

"It was foolish and not your decision to make!" I snapped. "He wanted to take you out but at least he came to seek permission. You, on the other hand, overstepped the commandments, and it was the wrong move on your behalf."

Guiseppe knew that he would have to be punished for his actions, not only for the murder but for disregarding the commandments. His consequences could have, and probably should have, been death, an eye for an eye, but I chose a punishment that, instead, would, forever, remind him of his error.

"Give me your arm," one of my enforcers commanded him and, needless to say, he was reluctant, given the vat of acid before him.

"Please, not this," Guiseppe pleaded in trepidation of the scorching that would soon take place. "I'd rather die."

I almost felt sorry for him but he had taken another man's life for causes of his own. My reluctant eyes were forced to watch his torment as the acid devoured his skin and the putrid smell seared my nose. He shrieked with pain and my ears burned at the sound. His torture was almost too much to bear and I was tempted, several times, to halt it. I battled to convince myself not to allow human compassion to overpower what had to be done, but my eyes struggled to observe. It was the exact reason that women were never accepted into this organization. There was no place for compassion or emotion when business needed to be handled, and it was definitely my biggest struggle.

It was several minutes later before his arm was brought out of the vat, his skin severely scalded and draped from the bone. I swore I could smell his rotted flesh and it made me sick to my stomach as I fought to maintain my composure. Guiseppe was a wounded child, a remorseful soldier, forced into submission with his weary, flooded eyes and flushed, sweating face. His melted flesh was cooled with water and he was sent on his way with a daunting lesson learned.

Still at hand was the property dispute between the two families, each relentless in its battle to retain what it, genuinely, believed its own. I ordered the heads from each family to meet with me, to settle the matter.

"The buildings are in our territory," Genovese informed.

"I paid for the property from Bianchi," Laruso argued.

"It wasn't Bianchi's to sell," Genovese replied.

"That's why we took him out," was Laruso's response.

"Enough!" I shouted. "Bianchi is dead now and one of your own had to pay for it so let's leave his name out of it." I turned to Genovese. "Did you see any of the money?"

"No, Capo, I didn't even know of the deal."

"Where's the proof that you paid for it?" I asked Laruso, and he produced a deed of ownership. "There it is, then," I concluded. "Laruso owns it."

"With all due respect, Boss, that paper didn't come from me," Genovese remarked. "I didn't approve that deal."

"Well, then, it sounds, to me like Bianchi might have been punished, anyway, for making deals behind his capo's back," I replied, confident with my decision.

I was uncertain but proud of the way that I had handled the dispute. Of course, my experience didn't match my father's, whose was extensive, but my decisions were being made based on the commandments of the Commissione and what I thought to be right in the honor of the organization. I tried to teach a lesson behind every punishment that I rendered and, as much as I loathed it much of the time, all of my reprimands were met with second guessing the penalties that I had handed down. The bosses before me had never, even once, struggled with it like I had and I knew that was their reason for barring women from their business. Women, of course, were too compassionate, lacking in the stoutness that it took to be a Mafiosi. I began to wonder if that was my problem, too. My punishments didn't display my sorrow but the afterthoughts following them tormented me. I found that I was good at making money and terrible at everything else, and it made me question what "the family" thought of me and my method of handling things. I was sure that at least some of them doubted my ability to be a capo and were waiting to see me fail.

Marco was slowly reentering my life and, though I should have been hesitant to accept his advances, my lonely nights shamefully permitted them. He had always been hard to resist, even during my relationship with Georgio. This time was no different, except that my desire for him was even stronger. There had always been an undeniable magnetism between us that I was sure would never fade. I was in love with him again, just as I had been since we met. He was married to his wife but dedicated to me. She had always known his love for me and it was the root of her abhorrence of me. The commandments prevented a divorce between them so she had the man and I had his devotion. All that I could ever do was love him. Anything else belonged to her, alone. It was no secret to her that his absence from home was time with me. It was understood that mafia men had mistresses. The younger women weren't flaunted in the faces of the wives but they were all aware of the affairs.

It became that Marco spent half of his weeks with his wife and the other half with me. Neither she nor I was content with the arrangement but we both accepted what we could get. The nights with my lover fulfilled me with romantic dinners and intimate massages, all free of our business matters. I relished his companionship, and it was the most complete that I'd felt since Georgio. Marco understood me. He respected my position and had aided in my transformation from a naïve teenager to a mature woman and dominant leader. He had seen me through the stages of my adult life and endured my love for another, his good friend, Georgio. Marco knew me like no other and he complimented my character. I wondered how it was that we had ever parted, to begin with and, at times, it felt as if we never even had. Still, I realized that I had become no better than the mistress of my father. I couldn't hold any grudges against my lover's wife because she felt the desperation of my mother, a woman pining for her cheating husband. Our affair was wrong, I knew, but I was already in too deep.

Emilio had gone from the stranger in town to more of a nuisance than I could have ever imagined and, no matter what I tried, I couldn't rid myself of him. His behavior was abnormal and something beyond merely a man's innocent admiration for a woman. His continuous phone calls and unanticipated appearances at the places I frequented were disheartening, to say the least, and his attempt at making it all seem coincidental was failing miserably. It seemed that I had become his focus, for whatever reason, and more than his interest in me was his concern with my activities. My suspicion of him was rapidly increasing.

"He's harmless," Gino responded to my weariness. "He's just hanging around as a friend, and he's one of us in America. You know how these guys are, Boss. It's respect by association. He wants people to see him as one of us." Emilio wasn't one of us and Gino knew better than to have him hanging around.

"I want Emilio checked out," I commanded of Mario. "Have your guys follow him for a while and see what he's about." It was imperative for us to deter outsiders from our world. We were heavily involved in a variety of activities throughout Italy and all over the world that only a select few fully knew about, even if they did know who we were.

It was no secret that our activities weren't exactly legal by Italian government standards. Everyone knew our reputation, and it was accepted because the Cosa Nostra was too big to bring down. We could conduct business from anywhere, including prison, if we needed to but, no matter what happened, our activities would continue. It was too profitable not to.

We had all sold our souls to the devil to play his game, and I found myself engulfed in atrocious things that I never anticipated. The admiration that I had always carried for my father was of his power and respect, but I never examined him enough to question how he earned it. The darker side of torture and murders that I was ordering so frequently had always been kept hidden within my father, away from my mother and away from me. I thought that, in time, it would all become second nature to me but it hadn't. I was just different. On the street, I saw men that were maimed, by my orders, and children who were left in the world without their fathers because I had ordered them killed. The battle with my conscience persisted but I always forced myself beyond it to perform my duty. Compassion had no place in our world but the consequences of my decisions weighed heavily on me and, often times, I doubted my abilities as a capo. Surely, everyone else doubted me too I thought, but if they did, no one ever uttered it to me.

Even after the death of my father, the family still gathered with my mother and me, weekly, as they always had, for social dinners and other occasions. They had been there my entire life. For us, it was tradition and nothing had changed, except for the absence of my father. The gossiping wives still gathered in the kitchen, preparing our meal, while the men sat with their Cuban cigars, telling their lame jokes. Just as when I was growing up, I still seemed the outcast, never fully belonging with either group, so I alternated time between the two, except for after dinner when I joined the men in the den, like my father always had. It was there that much of our business was discussed, a meeting of sorts. I thought back to how I had always yearned to be part of it growing up. They were sort of forced to accept my presence, but I felt like they were just as uncomfortable as I was there, often times. No matter how much I proved myself, women would never be truly accepted in their world, and I knew that the first chance one of them got to oust me, they would seize it.

Chapter 16

Emilio had been trailed by my guys for a couple of weeks when Mario and I met for a drink at a bar that we frequented.

"Did they get anything on him?" I asked, and his eyes confessed that they had. From a large envelope, he pulled out a stack of photos. A few were of Emilio meeting with Gino at various locations.

"Take a look at these." Mario presented photos of Emilio meeting with a man whom the organization knew very well. It was Howard Coran, who headed up the anti-mafia association in Sicily.

The Cosa Nostra had plenty of experience with the tough-talking, middle-aged pioneer. He had been on his mission to disband organized crime for years. I had to admire his courage to take on a group notoriously known to kill for the smallest of reasons. He was certain of his safety, aware that if he ended up dead or missing, the mafia would be looked at immediately.

The images of Emilio with him explained all of his obsessive behavior. He was just a pawn who Howard had set up to infiltrate the family for information. I was almost disappointed at how mindless and simple his game was. Emilio had granted us no challenge at all, and I thought our nemesis could have done better.

"I want Gino in here now," I demanded and sent Mario to find him. My suspicion was deep-seated that he had pumped Emilio with information that could wreck us. Already, I found myself plotting Gino's punishment because, in my heart, I knew he was guilty.

He arrived with discreditable eyes and a cowardly face, and they spoke of his betrayal. I was sure that he knew what I was about to confront him with. Beads of sweat dappled his forehead as I pulled the photos from the envelope. Without a word, I tossed them down in front of him, on the bar. Nothing needed to be said. The pictures explained themselves. In silence, I could see him searching his mind, desperately, for an adequate response that wouldn't be found. He borrowed his innocence.

"I swear, I didn't know," he insisted but my gut told a different story.

"Sure you did," I rebutted with conviction. "You knew."

"Fran, I swear, no. I wouldn't do that to the family."

"What does Emilio know?" Mario interrogated. "What does he know, scumbag?"

"Niente, nothing," he affirmed but it didn't add up.

"What does he know?" Mario demanded the truth with a blade to his throat. Gino ceased his breath with his eyes tightly shut. He knew that our threats were serious and that we wouldn't hesitate to act on them, especially since he, himself, had followed through on orders to punish or get rid of people who the organization deemed a problem.

"I swear, I don't know. Nothing from me, I swear. Please, don't," he pleaded vigorously. "I'm telling the truth."

It couldn't be denied that I was torn. Gino had been devoted to the family for years, my father's most trusted advisor. It was nearly impossible to believe that he was a rat. I wondered if he had been an informant all that time. Maybe he really wasn't guilty, I thought, and that the photos were just coincidental. It was my hope but, as much as he'd pushed Emilio on us, I knew that it wasn't the case. He was an informant. I thought about the weeks I had known Emilio. I thought back to his actions, searching for even one that might have proven him legitimate to us, any of the activities that the mafia was known for, but there were none.

"You know me," he said, pleading for his life. "You know me, Fran." I truly thought that I did but was forced to question my instincts. I wanted to have compassion for him but I couldn't. "I've been there since you were just a little girl."

"Here's the deal then," I told Gino. "If you're truly with us, then you can be the one to take out Emilio." It was a test of his loyalty, a sure-fire way to determine whose side he was really on. If he was a rat, there was no way that he would take Emilio out.

"I'll need to see his body. No fake pictures. I want proof, Gino." It was time for him to prove himself. Reluctantly, he agreed and was turned loose. I commanded Mario to have Gino followed, to detail his activities. As hard as it was to believe that he would betray us, my suspicion of him was overwhelming, and I feared the worst.

My mother hadn't been the same since my father died. She couldn't seem to recover from his death and my concern for her was growing. Her unending grief took over her ability to manage the restaurant, but she refused to sell the business that she had spent so many years building. I had been doing my best to keep the restaurant operating until I could find a replacement to manage it, which I found in Carmine's wife, Sophia. Along with her experience, my mother trusted her. Still, I was worried about her living alone in her mental state.

"Mama, why don't you stay with me for a while?" I pleaded with her, like so many times before, but my requests only offended her.

"I'm staying right here. This is my home and I'm not leaving it until I'm dead."

She was stubborn and determined but I knew that she just couldn't live alone any longer. Neither her mental nor physical health could endure it. She needed a companion to take away the depression she felt when she was alone. It was always my assumption that the restaurant would occupy her time and thoughts after my father's death but even it was no longer enough to fulfill her.

Against her will, I hired a woman to stay with my mother at night, when her friends and I were unable to be there. Stella was a middle-aged, Catholic nurse who spent time reading, playing cards, watching television or just talking with my mother. She had been hired to be my mother's new best friend and, though it began with a lot of resistance, the woman had grown on my mother.

I met with Mario for an update on Gino and Emilio.

"He says it's done," Mario said of them. We drove to an abandoned building, outside of town, where Gino sat in his dark-colored Lincoln. I held, tightly, to the gun holstered at my side, in case I needed it. In our world, no one could be fully trusted. Gino eased his way out of the car as I cautiously investigated our surroundings for anyone else who might be lurking. He opened the trunk and inside was Emilio, his hands and feet bound with rope and blood covering his head. He lay, motionless, with his eyes closed, and he appeared to be dead.

"I shot him in the back of the head," Gino announced in a quivering tone and he wreaked of perjury. I'd been around dead people enough to know that something just didn't look right.

"He's alive," I told Mario after detecting a pulse.

Pop! Pop! Mario fired two shots into Emilio's chest before firing two more into Gino. Both men lay dead, the result of their betrayal. We knew that there had to have been a witness or cameras hidden, some way for the pair to take us down, and we were prepared to take out anyone who stepped out of the shadows. Our search yielded several cameras, which were destroyed.

"Let's get them out of here," I commanded and Mario summoned his men to do the job. Both men became part of the concrete slab at Gino's new house being constructed.

I was disappointed with the outcome and had hoped that Gino was genuine. He had been like family to me for so many years, my whole life, and I grieved his passing. I held many memories of him in my head, times of sitting on his lap as a child while he sang to me, piggyback rides around my parents' house, telling stories at the dinner table. He had even taught me to drive a car. Gino had always been my favorite and someone I admired. Now, I had been forced to end his life and worse was the task I faced of telling his wife. Part of me already regretted my decision, but my priority was with the family and my job was to protect them at any cost.

I couldn't tell Gino's wife the truth about his death so I arrived at her house, later that day, with a fictitious story about him being missing and I hoped that it was believable enough. It brought back memories of the lie I had told my mother about my father's death.

"Missing?" Gino's wife echoed. "What are you saying?" Concern invaded her face.

"He's been wanting out of the organization for a very long time," I told her. "We believe the Sicilian government has him in hiding, possibly even as an informant." It was an outlandish fabrication that was hardly believable but it was all I had at that moment.

"He took off with her, didn't he?" She interrogated, angrily, referring to his long-term mistress. Her eyes became fiery swords with her suspicions. I felt sorry for her, this woman who felt scorned by her husband but was only betrayed by us, those who she considered her own family, the people she trusted most in the world. I needed her to have the dignity that she deserved.

"We don't think she had anything to do with it," I told her. "I know how much he loves you." She was wounded, like my mother, her heart in agony as she yearned for answers.

"Please let me know if there's anything I can do and I'll let you know if I hear anything else," I assured her, feeling guilty for my lie. Compassion, it was always the obstacle that kept me from being the capo that I needed to be. In my world, it wasn't a good quality to have, and I knew that if anything brought me down, that would be it.

Chapter 17

Needless to say, the murders of Gino and especially Emilio prompted an investigation from the Anti-Mafia Association. The men were suspected dead by the organization, but we knew that it could never be proven. Without a body, a man wasn't dead, only missing. It was the motto that we lived by. We were always careful to ensure that there was no body to be recovered. In our world, they were cut up, cemented in concrete, even eroded with acid but, with the exception of the few weighted down in the river, we never left any evidence of a murder.

Their investigation forced us to lay low for a couple of months and it nearly crippled our business. The Association monitored and appeared to analyze our every move. It was already obvious to us that Emilio and Gino had been feeding the Association information on our activities. What we didn't know was how much and for how long. I worried about how much they knew and what would be done because of it.

No matter how careful I made sure that all of us were at all times, I always had the feeling of being followed. I worried that I was being closely watched and that even my phone was tapped.

My privacy had been invaded and stolen by them.

I was jolted out of my first good night's sleep in weeks by the telephone ringing on the nightstand beside my bed.

"Francesca, your mother . . ." her nurse, Stella, frantically spoke on the line. Her voice held an urgency that hurled me into a whirlwind of panic. My mother's health had been steadily deteriorating since the death of my father. Her life without him had been a continuous battle. She had never been the same after losing him, and I blamed myself for taking his life and ruining hers. I rushed to the hospital, where Stella was waiting.

"The doctors are with her," the middle-aged caregiver informed me, gently, as a mother would her child. I saw anguish in her eyes. "She had a stroke. It doesn't look good, Francesca."

"It doesn't look good." Her words slammed me like a bullet through the chest, deafening my ears to only a shrill ringing. I swore that I felt the blood rush form my body as my surroundings spun, rapidly, in my fading vision until, suddenly, darkness.

"Francesca!" I heard, faintly, in my ears. "Francesca!" My name grew louder and it was as if I was dreaming. The sound of voices echoed around me. They spoke to me but I was unable to respond.

"Open your eyes," I heard one command of me and, slowly, I did. The blurred vision of people around me slowly cleared and I found Stella, Marco, and two others kneeling over me. I realized the chilliness of the tile floor beneath me.

"Are you alright?" A nurse, who looked to be in her twenties, asked me but I couldn't answer.

"Do you know where you are?" Stella inquired. I did know but I was unable to speak. I had no idea what had happened or how long I had lay there, but I knew that I was at the hospital to see my mother. Two nurses carefully helped me onto a sofa there, in the waiting area.

"Do you feel okay?" One queried.

"I think so." My words had finally returned as I tried to gather my thoughts together. "What happened?"

"You passed out and hit the floor," Stella responded.

"Smacked your head pretty hard, too."

"I don't feel anything," the nurse chimed in after examining my head. "Lie there and rest for a bit but don't fall asleep," she added.

"Mama!" The recollection of her ailment plagued my mind.

"She's still in with the doctors," Stella replied. I was controlled by a horrendous feeling of alarm and sorrow. The feeling that death was upon her inundated me.

"I have to see her," I asserted, attempting to rise up from the couch. There was a dire need to comfort my mother and tell her I loved her. I sensed that she needed me, and I wanted her to know that I was there. On the couch, I sat, lightheaded and fragile.

"We can't see her yet," Stella informed me but my determination argued otherwise. I rose up from the couch and stumbled down the hall to the doors of the emergency area.

"You can't go in there, signorina," a nurse halted me.

"Mia madre is in there and I need to see her!" My insistence didn't faze the nurse. "I want to know what's happening!" I ranted, hysterically, as Stella and Marco made their best attempts to calm me. I needed to know my mother's condition, immediately, and I threatened to bust through the secured double doors if I didn't get an answer.

"Calma, while I check to see what is going on with her," a nurse urged and I obeyed, taking deep breaths. The ghastly ache in my chest warned of bad news. I couldn't rid myself of the feeling that something was wrong. Only minutes later, a doctor followed the nurse back over to me. His facial expression screamed of tragedy.

"Your mother had a massive stroke," he spoke, softly. "We tried everything we could but weren't able to save her. Mi dispiace tanto."

The shock of his words jarred my body from the inside out as I struggled to grasp the notion of her being gone forever. I was angry, furious that she'd been taken from me, so suddenly, before I could even say goodbye, and I felt that it was the karma coming back on me for all that I had done to others. I felt that my mother's death was my fault and I wailed with guilt and grief as Marco held me in consolation.

"Would you like a minute with her?" The doctor asked and I followed him back to the petite room.

She lay, finally in peace, more serene than I'd ever seen her and, from it, I found my own reprieve. No longer would she be forced to endure the torment of her barren days without her husband.

"Now, you're with him again," I said as I held her hand in mine under the dimmed light. Tears flooded my eyes as I bid her farewell. "You were an amazing lady, Mama," I said. "I will miss you and honor you always." With a gentle kiss on her cheek, I said goodbye.

My mother's funeral was a parade of Mafiosi, relatives, local Sicilians, even political figures, most who knew her as my father's wife. She was well-respected for that reason, and hundreds arrived to offer their sympathetic farewells. She was adored by her community and would be sorely missed.

"She was a terrific lady," many complimented of her and it was true. I would never know another like her.

I peered down at her, in the white marble casket. She looked serene and it was comforting to know that she was finally at peace, with my father and with Jesus. Her troubles were gone and it lent me magnificent relief, but the agony of losing her remained. I didn't know how to live without her and it was then that I understand what she'd felt with the loss of her husband.

I realized that I'd grown to know death well. In the Cosa Nostra, we were encased in it so tightly that I almost didn't notice it anymore. Those people weren't my family. They weren't my friends. My mother's was a death that truly affected me to the core. It proved that my hardened heart could still feel. The pain was suffocating and it showed me that human life was valuable, that every life I took cursed someone with the grief that I felt for my mother. I was remorseful, sorry for the torment that I had bestowed on so many and I yearned to be forgiven. The compassionate side that I thought had always plagued me had been given to me by my mother. It had always been her gift to the world.

At the wake were officers of the Anti-Mafia Association, conspicuous spies of our activities. They knew of my mother being so closely connected to the organization and had expected the cosca there. With them, my informant, Antonio, stood, an observer of my grief. No one had ever seen me so fragile. The resilient capo, who had always disguised herself merciless, was a wounded child, my vulnerability exposed for the world to witness. It was unnerving and degrading but I didn't care that my reputation was uncovered. It was the first time that I could ever recall not caring about the family. They weren't my priority anymore. My mother's death made me realize that being a Mafiosi was no longer the life that I wanted. I needed a change, a chance at redemption for my transgressions.

After that day, I met with Antonio with a heavy heart.

"I'm walking away from the family," I told him.

"I guess, in a sense, you are," he replied, "but you're also finding your freedom." He smiled and I knew that he was right. "I know it's a hard decision but we're going to protect you, take care of you with a whole new life, away from Sicily and away from this."

"I just walk away, free and clear, huh? That's it?"

"That's it," he answered. I could board a plane and fly to freedom, no questions asked, no consequences rendered, just for leaving my life of crime. It seemed too good to be true.

"I want out," I informed the Commissione. It wasn't customary that one, especially in my rank, could simply walk away from the world we lived in.

"Do you know that there is a hit out on you?" One asked.

A member of my own cosca had placed a bounty on my head for my title. It was just a matter of time before I was done in by those under me. I was dumbfounded by their will to end my life so easily, with no regrets. Those who pretended to respect me were willing to betray me.

The Sicilian government had offered me immunity for ratting out other key players in the organization but I refused and, for that, the family was merciful, permitting me the exit that wasn't granted to Mafiosi wanting to leave the family and its activities. I was an enormous risk to them if I left but, in the end, I had earned their trust.

"You do understand that you can never return. You can't come back here for any reason and you will still be sworn to confidence by the omerta. You understand that, even outside of Sicily, we will locate and deal with you in any way necessary if you speak of the activities you have witnessed or been part of?"

"I understand," I assured them.

"Where are you going?" Marco probed when I informed him of my decision to leave the organization. I took a deep breath in the anticipation of opportunity.

"I don't know." I liked the sound of my statement.

"I'll go with you," he said but the truth was that I needed to leave him as well.

"You need to be with your wife, your family," I said, caressing hi cheek, "and I need to do this on my own," I added. "Sempre guardare la schiena, always watch your back, I told him and hugged him goodbye.

"Ladies and gentleman, please remain seated until the aircraft is in the air," the friendly voice of the airline stewardess announced as I settled in for my long flight. I stared out the window, breathing in freedom and stowing the memories of my former life. It was time to move on and I was ready for my rebirth.

"Brothers and sisters of our Father, God, in Heaven," I preached so proudly to the congregation of my church, "that is my story."

www.ingramcontent.com/pod-product-compliance
Lightning Source LLC
Chambersburg PA
CBHW051844170626
46807CB00003B/1335